W9-ACK-283

DATE

"Wake up, wake up; you've got to get in the shade!"

I shook my head and opened my eyes again. There was a man kneeling over me. He wasn't a native, and didn't suggest an explorer or a traveler. He was wearing a correctly tailored white morning suit, with pin-stripe pants, white ascot tie, and a white cork bowler.

"Am I dead?" I asked. "Is this Heaven?"

"No, my good man," he answered, "this isn't Heaven. This is the Pacific Island of Krakatoa."

"An absurd and fantastic tale. . . . Truth and fiction are cleverly mingled."
—*Library Journal*

SOME OTHER PUFFIN BOOKS YOU MIGHT ENJOY

The Twenty-One Balloons

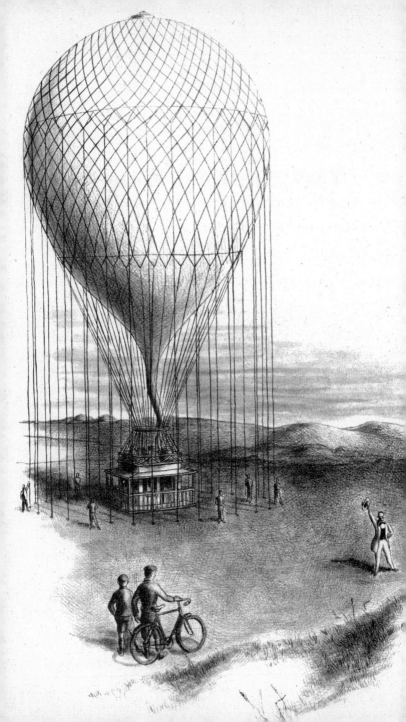

The
TWENTY-ONE BALLOONS

Written and illustrated by

WILLIAM PÈNE DU BOIS

PUFFIN BOOKS

PUFFIN BOOKS

A division of Penguin USA Inc.,
375 Hudson Street, New York, New York 10014
Penguin Books Ltd, 27 Wrights Lane, London W8 5TZ England
Penguin Books Australia Ltd, Ringwood, Victoria, Australia
Penguin Books Canada Ltd, 10 Alcorn Avenue, Toronto, Ontario, Canada M4V 3B2
Penguin Books (N.Z.) Ltd, 182–190 Wairau Road, Auckland 10, New Zealand
Penguin Books Ltd, Registered Offices: Harmondsworth, Middlesex, England

First published by The Viking Press, 1947
Published in Puffin Books 1986

50 49

Copyright William Pène du Bois, 1947
Copyright © renewed by William Pène du Bois, 1975
All rights reserved

Printed in U.S.A.

Set in Times Roman

Library of Congress Cataloging in Publication Data
Du Bois, William Pène, 1916–   The twenty-one balloons.
Reprint. Originally published: New York: Viking Press, 1947.
Summary: Relates the incredible adventures of Professor William Waterman Sherman,
who in 1883 sets off in a balloon across the Pacific, survives the volcanic
eruption of Krakatoa, and is eventually picked up in the Atlantic.
[1. Balloons—Fiction.   2. Voyages and travels—Fiction.   3. Krakatoa (Indonesia)—
Eruption, 1883]   I. title.   II. Title: 21 balloons
PZ7.D8527Tw   1986   [Fic]   86-42513   ISBN 0-14-032097-0

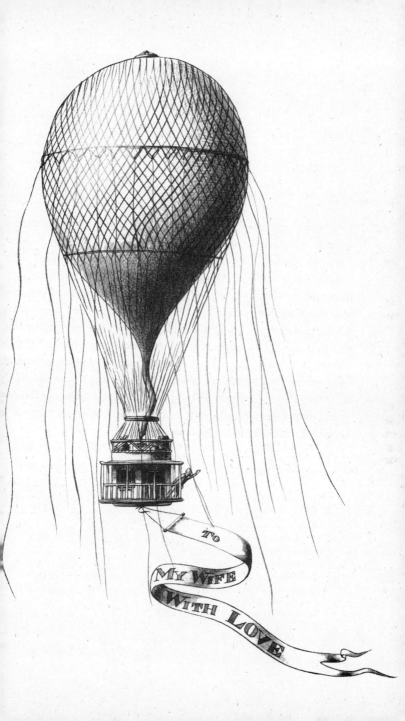

Author's Note

Just before publication of *The Twenty-One Balloons*, my publishers noted a strong resemblance between my book and a story by F. Scott Fitzgerald entitled "The Diamond as Big as the Ritz," published by Charles Scribner's Sons. I read this story immediately and discovered to my horror that it was not only quite similar as to general plot, but was also altogether a collection of very similar ideas. This was the first I had heard of the F. Scott Fitzgerald story and I can only explain this embarrassing and, to me, maddening coincidence by a firm belief that the problem of making good use of the discovery of a fabulous amount of diamonds suggests but one obvious solution, which is secrecy. The fact that F. Scott Fitzgerald and I apparently would spend our billions in like ways right down to being dumped from bed into a bathtub is altogether, quite frankly, beyond my explanation.

William Pène du Bois
January 16, 1947

Contents

Introduction

THERE ARE TWO KINDS OF TRAVEL. THE USUAL way is to take the fastest imaginable conveyance along the shortest road. The other way is not to care particularly where you are going or how long it will take you, or whether you will get there or not. These two methods of travel are perhaps easiest to be seen by watching hunting hounds. One hound will follow his nose directly to his prey. Another will follow his nose in a roundabout way to molehills, empty rabbit holes, garbage cans, and trees; and perhaps not pay any attention to his prey even when he happens upon it. This second way of getting around has always been pointed out as the nicest for, as you can see in the case of the slower hunting hound, you are able to see more of what is going on in the world and also how nature is getting along.

Not long from now, in the Atomic Age, it is easy to imagine that travel will be tremendously fast. In order to travel, for example, from New York to Calcutta, you will simply have to walk into a station in New York, through one door into a room beamed on Calcutta, out another door into the station in Calcutta, then on out into Calcutta's streets. It will take you no longer than it takes you to walk through any ordinary room and you won't feel a thing. What will happen when you enter the room is that you will be atomically broken down into a radio wave, transmitted by radio to Calcutta, and atomically restored upon being picked up by the radio receiver in Calcutta. The instant you are no longer in New York you will be in Calcutta in the same way as the instant a man's voice leaves a radio station it can be picked up anywhere in the world. Travel to any capital in the world will be instantaneous, for once man discovers the deeper secrets of nature, time and space will stop being paired together. You will hear of "miles" and you will hear of "hours," but the expression "miles per hour" will be most old-fashioned.

The best way of travel, however, if you aren't in any hurry at all, if you don't care where you are going, if you don't like to use your legs, if you want to see everything quite clearly, if you don't want to be annoyed at all by any choice of directions, is in a balloon. In a balloon you can decide only when to start, and usually when to stop. The rest is left entirely to nature. How fast you will go and where is left to the winds. It is a wonderful way to travel, particularly if you want to travel from your home to school. You get up early in the morning with your schoolbooks, climb into the basket, look in the direction of the schoolhouse, untie the ropes, and fly off. On your way many delightful things can happen such as:

a) the wind will be calm and you'll never get to school;

4

b) the wind will blow you in the wrong direction and take you fifty miles out into the country away from school, and

c) you might decide to play hookey, just once, and nobody can bother you in a balloon.

Then too, you might fly over a ball park on the way and change your mind as you make a quick descent onto the roof of the grandstand. Or if you pass any lakes on the way to school you can drop a line and do some fine fishing. Balloon travel is the best, particularly between home and school.

These ideas on travel went through the head of a rather nice old professor named William Waterman Sherman. Professor Sherman had been teaching arithmetic at a school for boys in San Francisco for forty years and was thoroughly tired of the idea. At first he thought of balloon travel only as a wonderful way of going to school because he was so tired of teaching. Then he thought of balloon travel as a way of spending a year of rest after retiring. At the age of sixty-six he stopped teaching, built himself a huge balloon, and filled the balloon's basket full of food. In this giant balloon he thought he could float around for a whole year, out of touch with the earth, with nobody to bother him and leaving his destination to the winds. This book, *The Twenty-One Balloons*, tells of his exciting trip. It is exciting, for he ran into trouble right away, including such disturbances as the greatest explosion in the history of the world. It also tells of just about every kind of free balloon travel known to man and of a few balloon inventions unknown until now. The period of the book is the period when balloons were most popular, 1860 to 1890.

Half of this story is true and the other half might very well have happened. Some of the balloon inventions in this book were actually built with success, some were designed by famous balloonists who didn't have enough money to build them and try them out. The others might easily have happened too.

The part about the Pacific Island of Krakatoa is true. There is a volcanic island of that name in the Pacific and it did blow up with the biggest explosion of all time so that it is now half as big as it was in 1883. Krakatoa was fourteen hundred feet above sea level before the explosion. After the explosion it was a submarine cavity with its bottom more than a thousand feet below the sea. The sound of the explosion was heard as far as three thousand miles away, which is the greatest distance sound has ever been known to travel. The violence of the eruption caused dust, ashes, and stones to be hurled seventeen miles high into the air. The black cloud of ejected material darkened an area with a radius of one hundred and fifty miles from the eruption. Waves generated by the explosion reached a height of fifty feet, destroying countless vessels, swamping and inundating and completely destroying villages on islands hundreds of miles away, and causing thousands of casualties.

This book is the story of Professor William Waterman

Introduction

Sherman's unusual voyage, of his fabulous friends and un-usual life on the Island of Krakatoa ending with the nois-iest day in the life of any man in history.

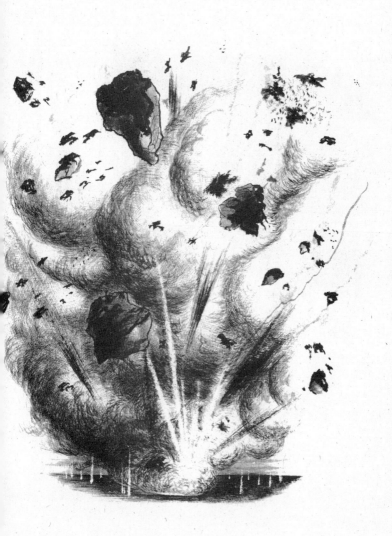

I

Professor Sherman's Incredible Loyalty

THE WESTERN AMERICAN EXPLORERS' CLUB, in the city of San Francisco, was honored as it had never been honored before in the first week of October 1883 by being promised to be first to hear the details of an unexplained, extraordinary adventure; the biggest news story of the year, the story the whole world was waiting impatiently to hear—the tale of Professor William Waterman Sherman's singular voyage. Professor Sherman had left San Francisco August 15. He flew off in a giant balloon, telling reporters that he hoped to be the first man to fly across the Pacific Ocean. Three weeks later he was picked up in the Atlantic Ocean, half starved and exhausted, clinging to the débris of twenty deflated balloons. How he found himself in the Atlantic with so many balloons after starting out over the Pacific with one, caught and baffled the imagination of the world. When he was sighted and rescued in the middle of the wreckage of twenty balloons in the Atlantic by the Captain of the freighter S.S.*Cunningham*, en route to New York City, he was immediately put to bed, for he was sick and weary, suffering from cold and shock. He was treated with great care by the ship's doctor, strengthened with food and brandy by the ship's cook, honored by the personal attention of Captain John Simon of the S.S. *Cunningham*. When he was well enough to talk, the Doctor, Cook, and Captain leaned over him at his bedside and said in excited voices, "How do you feel?"

"I could be worse," said Professor Sherman, rather feebly.

"Do you feel strong enough to tell us your story?" asked Captain Simon.

"I am strong enough," said Professor Sherman, "and I want first of all to thank you three gentlemen for your kind attention. But, gentlemen," he exclaimed, "as an honorary member of the Western American Explorers' Club in San Francisco, I feel sincerely that I owe the first accounting of my extraordinary adventure to that illustrious fraternity!"

At this, of course, Captain John Simon was somewhat hurt. After all, he had ordered the rescue of Professor Sherman when he found him floating around almost dead in a maze of broken planks and empty balloons, he had saved his life. And the ship's doctor had healed and tenderly nursed the Professor back on the road of recovery. The ship's cook had gone out of his way to prepare special, delicate food for him. They were all three most disappointed. This also made them much more curious. They tried all sorts of ways to get him to tell his story. They tried arguing

with, persuading, tricking, and agitating him. They tried to entice him with spirits. They gave him medicine which made him dopey. But he only seemed to become more and more firm as he exclaimed as loudly as his strength would permit, "This tale of mine shall first be heard in the auditorium of the Western American Explorers' Club in San Francisco, of which I am an honorary member!"

"Will you at least tell me your name?" asked Captain Simon. "So that I might make a proper entry and report of the rescue in the ship's log."

"That information I shall not withhold," said the Professor. "My name is William Waterman Sherman."

"And now one more question," said Captain Simon.

"*No more questions!*" interrupted Professor Sherman. "You will be well rewarded for rescuing me and my fare will be paid in full. I am saving every other detail of the voyage for the Western . . . "

"All right, all right," said Captain Simon. He left the

Professor's cabin, went to his own, and made the following entry in the ship's log:

Tuesday, September 8, 1883; n.lat.60°, w.long.17°; weather clear— At twelve noon, sighted strange wreckage in the distance. Approached it with caution. Found it to be a mass of broken wooden beams to which were attached twenty ascension balloons in various stages of deflation. In the middle of all of this flotsam there appeared to be a large furnace, painted red with gold trim. The furnace toppled over and sank before we were near enough to make out clearly what it could possibly be for. Clinging to a beam which was part of a balustrade we found a man, near exhaustion and suffering from cold and shock. This man's clothes, unlike those of most explorers or balloonists, seemed suited for fashionable evening wear. We picked up the man, questioned him at length when he was able to talk, but the only information we could get out of him was that his name was William Waterman Sherman. Orders have been given to treat Professor Sherman with the normal care and attention given a regular passenger of this ship. He shall be treated and billed accordingly.

Professor Sherman's Incredible Loyalty

When the S.S. *Cunningham* arrived in New York, Professor Sherman was still in no condition to get around by himself. He planned a few days' rest before boarding a train for San Francisco. He asked Captain Simon to help him get to a hotel. Captain Simon helped him into a carriage and took him to the Murray Hill Hotel. He saw that he got a room, wrote down the number of the room. He then went back to his ship, picked up his ship's log which he took to the offices of the *New York Tribune*. He knew the story of the rescue had news value and that he could sell it for a handsome price to this paper. The *Tribune* bought the story immediately, paid Captain Simon for this information, and sent two reporters to Professor Sherman's room at the Murray Hill at once. Of course Professor Sherman didn't like this idea at all. To all questions asked him by the reporters he replied, "Gentlemen, I am saving the extraordinary details of my voyage for a talk in the auditorium of the Western American Explorers' Club in San Francisco—you are only wasting your time and mine. Good day, gentlemen!"

The reporters were quite disgusted at this. They made the most they could of the information found in Captain Simon's log and printed whatever story they could make of it on the front page. The story, incomplete as it was, did attract considerable attention. The headline read: PROFESSOR SHERMAN FOUND IN ATLANTIC WITH WRECKAGE OF TWENTY BALLOONS, and the sub-headline read: *Refuses to Explain How or Why*.

The *San Francisco Tribune* naturally picked up this story,

with tremendous interest. They wired the information to the *New York Tribune* that a Professor Sherman had only recently attempted to fly the Pacific Ocean in one balloon. The *New York Tribune* looked in its picture files and found a picture of Professor Sherman taken at the Higgins Balloon Factory. They sent a photographer to the Murray Hill Hotel who (with considerable difficulty) took a picture of Professor Sherman. The following day the *New York Tribune* printed the two pictures side by side, to show it was quite the same man, in the front page with a headline which read: PROFESSOR SHERMAN IN WRONG OCEAN WITH TOO MANY BALLOONS, and the subheading: *Refuses to Explain How or Why*. These two stories were enough to excite the curiosity of millions, and Professor Sherman, in his bed at the Murray Hill, suddenly found himself to be the center of a considerable amount of the attention of the world. The Mayor of New York paid him a special visit. With all the pomp and ceremony that could possibly be displayed around the sick bed of a weary explorer in a hotel room, the Mayor presented the Professor with the Key to the City. Professor Sherman thanked him at length for this honor.

"And now," said the Mayor, "would it be too much to ask you in return to give to me, to New York, to the nation, to the world, the details of your amazing exploit?"

At this Professor Sherman exploded with anger. "*Out of my room, Your Honor!*" he shouted. "What matter of bribe is this, trying to buy my loyalty to the Western American

Explorers' Club with the Key to this City? Out of my room, I say, and take your friends, reporters, and photographers with you!"

The *New York Tribune* made much of this the next morning, carrying the story on the front page again with a banner headline which read: KEY TO CITY FAILS TO UNLOCK SECRETS OF SHERMAN'S VOYAGE.

By now the public's curiosity was at a fever pitch, and

The Twenty-One Balloons

the following morning Professor Sherman received a telegram which to a less extraordinary personage would have seemed to deserve far more undivided and humble attention. It was from the Secretary to the President of the United States. It was an invitation to the White House suggesting that this might be the ideal spot from which to reveal to the world the story which it was so impatiently waiting to hear. It requested that the Professor telegraph his reply. Professor Sherman dictated the following message, to be sent to the President's Secretary, without so much as a moment's reflection:

Dear Sir,

I appreciate the fact that the President's invitation amounts to what I should consider a Command Performance. However there is a code of ethics among explorers which I find myself at this particular moment unable to break. Had I a less fascinating story to tell, nobody, except my fellow explorers, would care where or when I gave account of it. The very fact that my adventure is so unparalleled multiplies the need that I keep true to my oath of membership and first share the details of my passage with my brothers of the Western American Explorers' Club in San Francisco.

Will you please convey to the President this message and my sincere thanks for the honor he has bestowed on me by sending me this gracious invitation.

William Waterman Sherman

Instead of being angry at this reply, the President showed that he well appreciated the Professor's loyalty to his club.

Professor Sherman's Incredible Loyalty

He had his Secretary send the following unprecedented wire to Professor Sherman:

Dear Sir,

The President understands exactly how you feel. However, in view of the fact that the world is waiting impatiently to hear your story, he has instructed me to place the Presidential train at your disposal with instructions to clear the lines between New York and San Francisco so that you may get there with all possible speed. He has been informed that you are resting up after your unfortunate crash into the Atlantic Ocean and do not feel quite well enough to travel at present. He assures you, sir, that you will be as comfortable in his car as you are in your hotel bedroom, and that all possible care and attention will be given you on your trip. If this is convenient, and he believes it surely is, an ambulance will pick you up this evening at eight o'clock to carry you in comfort to the train.

Please do not bother to convey your thanks to the President. He will eagerly await reports of your trip across the continent as the President and the world breathlessly stand by waiting to hear your story from the auditorium of the Western American Explorers' Club in San Francisco.

The Secretary to the President of the United States

Professor William Waterman Sherman left the Murray Hill Hotel that evening at eight o'clock, San Francisco bound, on the Presidential train.

William Pène du Bois

II

A Hero's Welcome Is Prepared

WHILE THE REST OF THE WORLD calmed down a bit, knowing that there would be no further news from Professor Sherman until after the full five days it would take him to cross the country by Presidential train, San Francisco became wild with excitement. There have been many instances of a home town giving its returning hero a rousing welcome. But never before had a returning hero placed so much attention on his home town. San Francisco's reaction to this was to prepare for Professor Sherman the most fabulous celebration imaginable. Professor Sherman was a balloonist. San Francisco went balloon crazy. The railroad station was swathed in bunting, flags, and miniature balloons. The avenue from the railroad station to the Western American Explorers' Club was lined with triumphant Corinthian columns, each surmounted by a brace of bright-colored miniature balloons. Ladies revived the balloon fashions in dresses which had been popular in France a hundred years before. Fat ladies gave up their diets. Everybody talked about "that round look."

The Twenty-One Balloons

Balloons were the decorative scheme in all stores. In a fruit and vegetable store, for example, honeydew melons with a quart box of strawberries hanging from them by numerous strings were made to resemble ascension balloons and hung from the ceiling next to watermelon dirigibles and summer-squash blimps.

A Hero's Welcome Is Prepared

The Mayor of San Francisco ordered and had the City pay for one thousand miniature balloons to be used to decorate the avenue from the station to the Club, and the Municipal Buildings. He gave the contract for this big job to the Higgins Balloon Factory, thus honoring the workshop which built Professor Sherman's original giant balloon. These miniature balloons were made of silk, filled with hydrogen, and had a lifting pull of sixty pounds each. In an all-out effort of hard day-and-night work, the Higgins Factory finished the balloons in two and one half days. They were beautiful, painted many different colors, and shaped exactly like Professor Sherman's balloon though considerably smaller. By noon of the third day they were being attached to the various Municipal Buildings and along the avenue and looked very fine indeed.

The workmen who were attaching the balloons were followed wherever they went by bands of curious children who asked many questions about the balloons, particularly concerning what would be done with them after the parade. When the workmen had finished, one boy carefully watched them walk off down the road, then climbed up on the roof of the Post Office, untied a balloon, and excitedly brought it down to the street. The boy weighed about seventy-five pounds. The balloon had a lifting pull of sixty pounds. He wasn't strong enough to play around with it very much. As a matter of fact, all he seemed to be able to do was to walk around, stretched quite tall, on his tiptoes with his hands way above his head. Then he got an idea.

He tied the end of the rope around his waist, ran down the street with the wind, and jumped as high as he could in the air. The balloon carried him about the height of a second-story window and he floated down the street for half a block. This was fun. He tried it again. This time with a little more wind and a slightly bigger jump, he reached the height of a third-story window and flew a whole block. Of course about twenty children chased him down the street, all yelling and wanting to try to make a few leaps. He jumped down a few more blocks and by this time his arms were tired and his waist was sore, so he had to take a rest. He decided to let his younger brother have it next. His younger brother was quite a bit smaller and weighed about fifty-eight pounds. He grabbed the balloon as his brother wrapped the end of the rope around his middle, took a little jump, and sailed off very very slowly down the block. "He's better than you are," yelled one of the boys. "Look, he's four stories high and he's on his second block." Fortunately there was a church at the end of the street or the younger brother's leap might have turned out to be altogether too big. He managed to wrap his legs around the very top of the steeple, untie the balloon which shot upward into the skies, and grab the steeple with his arms and hang on as tightly as he could. He was yelling and screaming for dear life. Ten minutes later the Fire Department rescued the young boy, and the children decided to give up the balloon leap game.

The Fire Department, by the way, was kept pretty busy

all night. Sparks from chimneys would land on the small balloons along the triumphant avenue to the Explorer's Club causing them to blow up. There were no actual house fires; the balloons would flare up and disappear immediately, leaving no trace or fire. The resulting huge blazing flashes of light scared the people who lived in near-by buildings so much that they complained to the Mayor. The Mayor ordered the entire Fire Department to station all of its trucks and engines along the avenue and keep a sharp lookout all night. This reassured the people who lived near the decorated buildings, and they gradually, family by family, went to bed and eventually to sleep.

What was in a way the funniest incident resulting from the Mayor's plan to decorate parts of San Francisco with balloons caused considerable excitement some two hundred miles away. It started in San Francisco. The Mayor ordered workmen to decorate the cupola of the Western American Explorers' Club with ten alternating red and white balloons around its base, and one larger blue balloon with white stars attached to its very top. The cupola of the Club was an unusual piece of architecture. It wasn't actually in the original plans for the building. It was shaped like the upper half of the world, from the Equator at its base to the North Pole at its peak. There was a flagpole at this pinnacle from which waved the American Flag above, and the Western American Explorers' Club banner directly underneath. Maps of North America, Europe, maps of everything north of the Equator, were painted with care in gold and blue paint on the cupola. This unusual cupola was made of wood and had been firmly attached to the building twenty-three years after the building was completed. It was added with reverence and ceremony and it symbolized the Club's greatest ambition, to furnish the first expedition to plant the American Flag on the heretofore unexplored North Pole.

The ten miniature balloons around the base of the cupola had a combined lifting pull of six hundred pounds. The larger balloon attached to its top had a lifting pull of three hundred pounds. This made a total strain of nine hundred pounds. The cupola weighed a little over four hundred. Nothing unusual happened at first, but during the night, as the winds gently tossed the balloons back and forth, the cupola started to loosen somewhat like a tooth does. As night wore on, it became looser and looser. At one-twenty-nine o'clock in the morning, it gently rose from its perch on the Explorers' Club and, dropping bits of plaster, spikes, and rivets, flew off eastward over the city. It gained altitude and crossed mountain-tops without incident. It started losing altitude only after having had a nice flight of four and a half hours and landed silently and gracefully in a peaceful little Indian Reservation which was situated in a snug valley between two huge mountains.

As dawn came up and daylight began to appear in this valley, the Indians arose, walked out of their tents, and, beating their chests, took deep breaths of fresh air. *But what was this!* Right in the middle of the Reservation,

A Hero's Welcome Is Prepared

lined up with the other tents, was what appeared to be a small planet sunk in the ground and surrounded by smaller planets.

Now what do you suppose the Indians did?

Did they back away trembling with fear?

No.

Did they shriek with fright?

No.

Did they beat up the Medicine Man?

No. They gave the cupola an appraising look, then one of them said, "Huh! Dumb white man decorate Explorers' Club of San Francisco with too many balloons. Get hatchet. Cut door in United States between New York and San Francisco. This make good new house for Chief."

The Twenty-One Balloons

When the Mayor gave the miniature balloon contract to the Higgins Balloon Factory, he was rewarding a company which was near to Professor Sherman's heart. This was a nice idea. However, the Tomes Aeronautical Studios which were the San Francisco rivals to the Higgins Factory weren't at all pleased by his decision. At a time when San Francisco was balloon crazy, they found themselves to be sadly neglected. "Something has to be done, something unusual in the balloon line," said Joseph Tomes, the company's President. He immediately called a conference. The Directors thought hard, did much scratching of their heads and made many ridiculous suggestions, but were unable to think of any satisfactory ideas on such short notice. Somebody suggested that they look through their file of patents for some discarded invention of an earlier day. This seemed a good idea at such a pressing moment. After much study of all sorts of rare balloon inventions they found a suggestion in a pocket of the files marked "Ideas to be Considered." It quoted Benjamin Franklin in 1789, a year before he died. He was too sick at the time to stand the shocks and bumps of any form of travel. "I wish I had brought with me from France," Benjamin Franklin said, "a balloon sufficiently large to raise me from the ground. In my malady it would be the most easy carriage for me, being led by a string held by a man walking on the ground."

"*That's it!*" shouted Joseph Tomes. "Professor Sherman is sick. We shall build him a balloon carriage to carry him in comfort from the railroad station to the Explorers'

Club." The Directors agreed that here was a wonderful idea.

"But it lacks grace and isn't imposing enough," suggested one of the Directors, "and besides, the Mayor would never approve of a carriage in which there was no seat for him."

"The Mayor could be the man who walks on the ground and pulls the string," said Joseph Tomes, President of Tomes Aeronautical Studios.

"I do believe," the other Director argued, "that if we are to put on any sort of a show in this balloon-conscious parade, we shall have to do something more spectacular than that. I am only thinking out loud," he said in the manner of a man who is afraid of his own ideas, "but what do you think of this? We'll take a large, deep leather couch big enough to accommodate both the Professor and the Mayor. We will raise this just off the ground with two of our Number 3B Touring Balloons. To this comfortable floating couch we will harness three horses in single file. A postillion in a balloonist's suit will ride the front horse, thus directing our balloon buggy down the boulevard to the Explorers' Club."

"*That's it!*" shouted Joseph Tomes again. "A wonderful idea and it won't take any time to build. We have the balloons in stock. The couch in my office will do nicely." He then instructed one of the Directors to hire the horses and arrange some sort of steady harnessing so that the couch wouldn't tip. He instructed another to have two of the

27

Proposed "Tomes-Carriage"

Number 3B Touring Balloons filled with hydrogen and have the words, "WELL DONE, PROFESSOR SHERMAN" painted on them. "This fabulous balloon buggy," said Joseph Tomes, "should be ready by four this afternoon and I shall drive in it at that time with the Director who invented it to the City Hall where we will demonstrate it to the Mayor. Good day, Gentlemen."

The meeting thus came to an end.

While this excitement and hard work was going on at the Tomes Studios, the rest of San Francisco was beginning to calm down. This was September 22nd, the day be-before Professor Sherman was expected. San Francisco was all ready, the decorations were installed, the cupola of the Explorers' Club had mysteriously disappeared, and the Fire Department was getting ready to begin its second sleepless night protecting the houses along the avenue from exploding balloons. The people were getting quite restless and impatient. Their first enthusiasm was wearing off. They began wondering whether or not Professor Sherman was really worth all this bother and excitement. All they actually knew about him was that he wouldn't tell his story anywhere except in San Francisco. This was enough to make the world extremely curious, but was it enough to make Professor Sherman a hero? The people were beginning to lose interest. Some even decided they wouldn't bother to push their way through the crowds on the avenue to see him as he drove from the station to the Club. Then a young boy came to the Professor's rescue. He had just finished reading an extraordinary account of a trip by some intrepid adventurers. This trip had caused considerable stir, so much so that a well-known author of the times had written a book about it, calling the book *Around the World in Eighty Days*. This young boy started thinking about Professor Sherman's voyage. He had left San Francisco at three o'clock August 15th. He was later picked up with twenty balloons in the Atlantic. This meant he must have flown over parts of Asia and most of Europe too. He was rescued by a freighter and taken to New York. He was now being rushed from New York to his starting point, San Francisco, in the Presidential train. "If he arrives at three o'clock, on time, at the station in San Francisco," the young boy reasoned, "he will have traveled around the world in forty days and cut the old record in half." Everybody recognized the logic in this and new interest in the Professor spread all over San Francisco. Whatever other secrets he was saving for San Francisco, the fact remained that that record of long standing, around the world in eighty days, was to be decisively beaten by Professor William Waterman Sherman of the Western American Explorers' Club when he arrived the following day.

At four o'clock, back in the Tomes Balloon Studios, the "balloon buggy" was completed and Joseph Tomes and his enterprising Director climbed into the leather couch. A messenger boy was sent ahead to tell the Mayor to stand on his balcony at City Hall to see the arrival of this magnificent and most comfortable carriage. Joseph Tomes told the postillion to drive on. "We're off!" he shouted, and nervously sat back. This invention worked like a dream. The usual bumps you feel in carriages just didn't exist. Joseph Tomes and the Director took turns at patting each other on the back. "We'll sell a million of these," said Joseph Tomes. As they approached City Hall, Joseph Tomes and the Director leaned way back in the couch and crossed their legs. To show how completely at ease and comfortable they were, Joseph Tomes lit a cigar. This was a great mistake. As the balloon buggy floated up in front of City Hall, a spark from Joseph Tomes' cigar lit on one of the balloons. There was a tremendous explosion, a blinding flash, and Joseph Tomes and the Director fell rudely on their behinds and did backward somersaults on the pavement.

"*Please, Gentlemen!*" said the Mayor angrily. "On this of all days, I cannot waste my time with acrobatics."

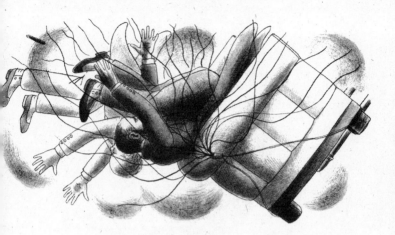

Joseph Tomes and the Director sadly walked back to the balloon factory as the three horses, scared by the explosion carried the postillion and dragged the couch on a wild three-mile gallop through the city's streets.

There were no further incidents to spoil the Professor's celebration. The following morning, there were still nine hundred and twenty-nine of the original thousand miniature balloons. A huge crowd gathered early along each side of the avenue of triumph. The Mayor gave final instructions to the official welcoming committee. He asked them to wear derby hats instead of the usual silk hats; and polka-dot ties, instead of the usual gray ascots. "This," the Mayor explained, "is so as to be in keeping with the balloon motif."

At exactly 2:56 o'clock on the afternoon of the 23rd of September the Presidential train was sighted in the distance and a gigantic cheer of welcome was heard from the people of San Francisco.

William Pène du Bois

III

A Description of the Globe

THE PRESIDENTIAL TRAIN ANSWERED THE CHEER OF welcome given it by the people of San Francisco with a long piercing toot. Then, pulling up at the station, it slowed down to a stop, panting and letting off steam as would any engine that had just completed a cross-country run. The Police Department had detailed one hundred officers to keep the station platform clear. These policemen interlocked their arms, forming a human chain which held the eager crowds back. The Presidential train was shorter than usual for greater speed and was made up only of an engine, coal tender, dining car, and the President's own car with the familiar observation and speech platform at the rear. The Mayor had the carriage, which was to take Professor Sherman to the Western American Explorers' Club, pull up opposite the Presidential coach, clapped his white gloved hands twice, and instantly two porters appeared with a red carpet strip which was rolled up like a huge jellyroll. He clapped his hands again and the red carpet was rolled across the station platform from the Professor's carriage to the President's coach. He clapped his hands again and the official welcoming

committee lined up on both sides of the carpet strip, wearing their smart bowlers and polka-dot ties. The Mayor then reached in his vest pocket, and took from there a small silver whistle which he tooted once. He replaced the whistle, then followed by the Chief Surgeon of the San Francisco General Hospital, he walked up the red carpet into the Presidential train. The whistle toot was evidently the cue to start the music by the combined Fire and Police Department bands, for instantly lovely strains of music were heard. As Professor Sherman, looking rather haggard and worn, descended from the train onto the red-carpeted platform with the Mayor holding him up on one side and the Chief Surgeon holding him up on the other, a medley of three appropriate songs was heard, mingled with the tremendous cheers from the crowd. These three songs, selected by the Mayor himself, were, *Oh When I Walk, I Always Walk with Billy; Billy Boy;* and *Marching Through Georgia.* It was thought afterwards by many that the slim connection between that last song and Professor William Sherman was a bit far-fetched.

Professor Sherman was assisted into the back seat of the carriage and the Mayor climbed in and sat beside him. The Chief Surgeon, acting as a sort of official footman, sat next to the coachman while, instead of lackeys, two trained nurses sat on the raised seats behind and overlooking the Professor. The carriage proceeded up the triumphant avenue from the station to the Explorers' Club through thunderous cheers and showers of confetti. Just as the carriage pulled up in front of the Club, a sweet-looking well-scrubbed little girl in a crisp white starched dress, an orphan from St. Catherine's Waif Home, rushed up to the Professor, curtsied politely, and presented him with a little bouquet of toy balloons. The Professor accepted the bouquet, thanked the little girl, and, as the crowd sighed its approval, kissed her on both cheeks. He was then helped out of the carriage, helped up the stairs into the Club, up the aisle which parted the packed auditorium in the middle, onto the speaker's platform where a freshly made bed awaited him. The Professor sat on the bed as the Chief Surgeon removed his shoes. He then swung his feet around up on the bed as the Chief Surgeon covered his lap with a comforter. Then, facing the audience, propped up in bed by one bolster and four huge pillows, Professor William Waterman Sherman was ready to tell his story.

"Ladies and Gentlemen, I have the honor to present Professor Sherman," announced the Mayor.

"Mr. Mayor, Fellow Explorers, Ladies and Gentlemen," said Professor Sherman. A hush fell over the audience. There was a small creaking sound of people getting themselves comfortably set, and then silence. "I am happy to be home again!"

At this, the audience rocked the building with cheers. The hubbub lasted four minutes before the crowd settled down again.

"I haven't been away very long, but I have certainly missed . . ."

The audience, reminded by this remark that the Professor had clipped forty days off the speed record for a trip around the world, broke out in tumultuous applause. This time it lasted five full minutes. The Professor looked helplessly at the Mayor who immediately sensed how he felt. He faced the audience, silenced it, and said, "Ladies and Gentlemen, Professor Sherman has a long and, we feel sure, interesting story to tell. He hasn't had a chance to say twenty words yet, and you have already interrupted him with ten minutes of applause. The Professor isn't running for President, he is recounting a scientific adventure to a scientific club. Kindly refrain from applauding hereafter until the Professor has concluded his story, thereby respecting the Professor's story and his ill health. Thank you."

The crowd responded to this by being absolutely quiet. Professor Sherman turned to the Mayor, thanked him with a nod, and started again:

It is funny that my trip has ended by being such a fast trip around the world. I find myself referred to now as one of the speediest travelers of all times. Speed wasn't at all what I had in mind when I started out. On the contrary, if all had gone the way I had hoped, I would still be happily floating around in my balloon, drifting anywhere the wind cared to carry me—East, West, North, or South. It just happened, by some strange fate, that the wind blew me three-quarters around the world at tremendous speed, and my only moments of rest were once when I crashed in the Pacific, and again after a crash in the Atlantic. The other reason why I took this trip was that I wanted to be alone, detached from the earth, in a balloon. But this didn't work out either. My trip wasn't half over when I found myself in a balloon contraption with eighty other people, men, women, and children.

For years I had cherished the idea of this trip. As you know, I was a teacher of arithmetic for forty years. Forty years of being surrounded by a classroom of healthy prank-ish students. Forty years of spitballs. Forty years of glue on my seat, Sal Hepatica in my inkwell, and other devilish tricks. Long about the thirty-sixth year, I started yearning to be alone. I amused myself with thinking of many ways of doing this, trips in small boats, Polar expeditions; I joined this Explorers' Club, for after all it seemed to me that the ambition of explorers was to go where no one had gone before. One day I started thinking of a balloon in which I could float around out of everybody's reach. This was the main idea behind my trip: to be where no one would bother me for perhaps one full year; away from all such boring things in the lives of teachers as daily schedules, having to be in different classrooms at exact times week after week.

I planned and worked on designs for my balloon in my spare time, using the experiments of other balloonists as a guide. I wanted a big balloon, one which could keep me in the air for a year, or at least many months. Big balloons are a problem. Unless they are designed with great care they are ripped to shreds by the wind while they are being inflated. Once a balloon is in the air, it offers little resistance to the wind and isn't bothered by it; but while it is tied down on the ground and being filled up with hydrogen it is at the wind's mercy. I followed the plans of the great French balloonist, Giffard, whose captive balloon, the *Clou*, is the biggest balloon ever built. His balloon was constructed of seven alternating thicknesses of rubber and silk. I planned my balloon, which I christened the *Globe*, with four alternating thicknesses of rubber and silk. My balloon was six thousand cubic yards in size, which is just about ten times the size of a standard balloon. The *Globe* was one of the biggest free balloons ever built.

A Description of the Globe

I wanted a big balloon for two reasons. First of all, as I have already said, to keep me in the air for a long time. My second reason was that I wanted a big basket to live in and it would take a huge balloon to lift the basket I had in mind. As you know, the standard balloon basket is just a little compartment about big enough for two men to stand in, or one man to sit down in, and altogether impossible to sleep in. There is little room for provisions and it would be impossible to live in a standard balloon basket for any length of time. This goes without saying. I looked to the work of another French balloonist named Nadar. Nadar built himself a big balloon which he christened *Géant* and attached to this a real little basket house. It had a door, windows, a staircase which led up to its little roof. The roof of the house was bordered by a woven balustrade, furnished with wicker furniture, and was an ideal observation platform. The inside of the house was appropriately and comfortably furnished. This was a basketweaver's masterpiece. It was light, strong, and comfortable. I designed my basket house in much the same manner with but few changes. I didn't use the roof of my woven house as an observation platform but rather as a sort of open-air attic in which to store food. For observation, there was a small porch all the way around my house with light uprights and balustrade made of bamboo. This porch was quite like the deck of a ship.

Nadar's balloon wasn't built, as mine was, with the idea of taking very long trips or staying in the air many months.

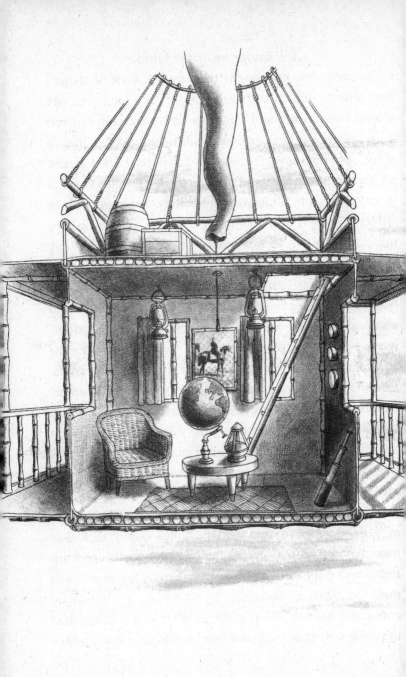

A Description of the Globe

He therefore didn't have to worry much about ballast. The way you take an ordinary trip in a balloon is quite simple. The balloon is tied down with several ropes while it is being filled with gas. When it is full, you give the command to cut the ropes and you fly off. The balloon will instantly leap into the air and carry you high up in the sky, the height depending on the amount of gas in the balloon and the amount of weight you are carrying. When you want to come down, you pull a rope which lets some of the gas out of the bag. If you want to climb higher, you must throw something overboard which will make the balloon lighter. Nadar carried bags of sand which he threw overboard when he wanted to gain altitude. Sand is the usual ballast used by all balloonists. I couldn't afford to use sand as ballast because in order to stay up in the air and live comfortably for a long period of time, I had to make every ounce I carried with me count. I used food for ballast. I thought this to be ideal for a long trip. With food for ballast, every time I threw a pail of garbage overboard, I would go a little higher. Thus for every unnecessary sandbag, I could carry extra food to make my trip last longer.

My balloon house was furnished with the lightest of everything. The usual mattress is too heavy and is only used at night anyway. I designed a mattress made of the same material as my balloon and filled with gas. With a sheet over it, it stayed on the floor and was most soft and comfortable. When I pulled the sheet off, it floated up to the ceiling and was thus stored out of my way in the daytime. I had chairs and a table made of balsa wood and bamboo. I had a library of paper-bound books printed in small type. My foods and liquids were chosen with the idea of saving weight. I carried a strong shark-fishing rod with the hope of catching a few fish to increase my food supply.

Some balloonists who recently planned ocean voyages, such as the Americans John Wise and T. C. Lowe, attached lifeboats to their balloons in case of a crash in the water. I couldn't see carrying this extra weight. I had a tailor make me two waterproof suits out of balloon cloth and carried a cork lifesaver. If I crashed, I figured that this type of suit would keep me dry, and the lifesaver would keep me above water. These suits were wonderful. They were light, and being both waterproof and airtight, were extremely warm. I planned to wear one and wash the other by attaching it to my shark-fishing rod and dunking it in the ocean. All of my laundry was done in this manner. The rest of my clothes were simply the lighter variety of everyday men's wear.

The Higgins Balloon Factory took a year to build my balloon, and I must say they made a fine job of it. It was finished August 10th of this year. I had one excellent trial flight in my balloon which I thought was enough. It was a short flight and everything worked perfectly. The only mishap was that I broke every plate and glass in my woven house when I came down a little too fast. I corrected this by having silver plates made to replace dishes, and used a silver cup instead of glasses. The plates and cup had small handles on them so that I could tie them onto my fishing rod and wash them by dunking them in the ocean.

I spent two days in outfitting my balloon with the proper provisions. I carried a small still for making fresh water out of salt water, and a medium sized keg of quinine tonic. I was soon all set for my trip.

Higgins notified the press that I had intentions of taking a long trip in a giant balloon which might easily end up in my being the first to fly across the Pacific Ocean. The newspapers carried the story, giving it about half a column on the fourth page. The public wasn't at all interested in my trip then. I think it was because Higgins told the newspapermen that my balloon wasn't quite as big as Nadar's. The public had heard of Nadar's giant balloon and, I'm sure, would have been curious to see it. But mine, which was just a shade smaller, was looked upon as just a runner-up.

As I sailed away August 15th at two o'clock in the afternoon, I was amused to see that only four of my closest friends were on hand to see me off. I told them I would be up for a year. Well, that's the way I had planned it then. I waved goodbye and gave the command to "Let 'er go!"

IV

The Unwelcome Passenger

WHEN RELEASED, MY BALLOON instantly and gracefully rose to a height of sixteen hundred feet, and kept this altitude as a swift wind carried me out over San Francisco and over the Pacific Ocean. Before taking off, I had lain down on my balloon mattress on the floor of my basket house and held tightly to two handles attached to the floor to bolster myself against the shock of a quick ascension. The first jolt was quite a large one, but as soon as the *Globe* reached its cruising altitude, which seemed to take only a minute or two, my flying basket house was as calm and easy to move around in as if it were on the ground. I swallowed several times to clear my ears because they felt stuffed up while the balloon was climbing fast. I got up off my mattress, straightened some books which had fallen from their shelves, and walked out on my porch to have a last look at San Francisco. It was a clear sunny afternoon, and I must say the city beneath me looked most beautiful. I noticed quite a few people looking up at me. Evidently the actual sight of my giant balloon and basket house was considerably more exciting to see than pictured

in the newspaper stories. I even noticed crowds of people running down the streets in the same direction that I was flying, so absorbed at looking up at me that they kept bumping into other people at street intersections. There was considerable confusion and even what appeared to me to be a street fight. This was most flattering.

The Unwelcome Passenger

In less than ten minutes, I was out over water and watching the coastline disappear from view. Several sea gulls were following the *Globe* as it flew off over the Pacific. Some of them rested occasionally on the balustrade around my porch, making my balloon descend a little; some of them rested on the silken surfaces of the balloon itself, which gave me some cause to worry. I knew the cloth, which was specially prepared and made to withstand tremendous punishment of all kinds, wouldn't be damaged by the gulls. But the sight of the birds, their sharp claws extended, coming in for a fast landing on my huge balloon, scared me to death.

Mariners have often told me that they consider sea gulls to be good luck and always feed them by throwing garbage overboard. I didn't have any garbage at that early stage of my trip and couldn't afford to spare any of my precious food for feeding birds so I had to risk misfortune and let the gulls go hungry.

My balloon house was nice to travel in, for except at noontime, when the sun was directly overhead, there was always one side of the porch where I could sit in the warm sun. I did a great deal of reading. Seated in a comfortable chair, my feet propped up on the balustrade—this was a truly enjoyable mode of life.

(At this last remark of Professor Sherman's, the other explorers in the well-behaved audience couldn't restrain a deeply felt sigh.)

I saved all of my garbage for the first three days, storing

it up front where the wind would carry its odor off ahead
of the balloon. On the morning of the fourth day, I must
say the odor from this garbage was becoming quite un-
bearable. The wind, of course, is always behind you when
you fly a balloon; and since the wind travels faster than the
balloon, due to the friction present when such a massive
body moves through the atmosphere, it carries all odors
forward. However, the odors from my garbage had become so persistent by the fourth day, that I was finding
myself to be constantly flying through my own smells, as it
were—a most disagreeable state of affairs. But then something truly wonderful happened. Rain clouds formed directly above me, that morning of the fourth day, and it began to rain and the wind blew the rain against my wicker
house making things generally unpleasant. This was excuse
enough to unload my food ballast. Holding my nose with

one hand, I walked up front and dumped all of the garbage over the side. The *Globe* instantly bounded up through the rain clouds, into the sun again, and I continued on in fresh air and sunshine. As I looked down at the rain clouds and took deep breaths of fresh air, I felt that I had indeed mastered the elements to a most satisfactory degree.

Night time in my balloon house was particularly enjoyable. The gentle motion of the balloon and my soft inflated mattress made a combination for perfect sleeping. I spent the early evening on my porch in solitary contentment, studying the stars. I think I can honestly say that my few days flying over the Pacific in the *Globe* were the happiest days of my life.

Everything worked pretty much as planned on the first few days of my trip. Doing my laundry and washing my dishes by dunking them at the end of my fishing line was fairly satisfactory. Reeling in a wet suit was quite tiresome, but I was invariably pleased to find my suit nearly dry by the time I had pulled it in. Fishing was poor from such a height. To reel in a fish at the end of a fourteen-hundred-foot line was too tricky for a fisherman of my caliber, and I dropped many of them long before I could even distinguish what kind of a fish I had hooked. I exercised by walking around the porch of my house—that is, I exercised my legs in this manner. My arms got plenty of exercise reeling in the laundry and dishes.

I sighted a small fishing boat in the afternoon of the fifth day. This was the first sign of life I had seen since leaving San Francisco. I soon noticed that I was going to fly directly over it, so I decided to try and signal it. I knew a little Morse code, so I took a mirror and flashed the message, "I am Professor Sherman of San Francisco and all is well." The fishing boat, manned evidently by a Japanese crew, slowly flashed back the simple message, "No speak English." This to me was just right. I wanted to be alone, out of touch with the world. This was the first sign of life I had seen in five days and it couldn't possibly contact me. All was indeed well.

The sixth day was perfect: calm and uneventful. My garbage was again beginning to make its presence felt, but it wasn't too bad.

The seventh day, Ladies and Gentlemen, was catastrophic!

I shall never forget the seventh day of this voyage of mine for as long as I live. Just about everything went wrong, and my dreams of spending a year in a balloon were shattered. The first thing I noticed on the morning of that fateful day was a small speck far off on the horizon which couldn't possibly be anything else but land. Land on my seventh day out—I had flown straight across the Pacific Ocean at a fabulous rate of speed! I had originally hoped that the winds would blow me first in one direction and then in another and that I would spend at least a month without seeing any land whether it be on the Asiatic side of the ocean or back on the American side. But there in the distance before me was a small speck which was slowly taking on the shape of a little volcanic island, most of it mountain, with a column of smoke slowly rising from it into the blue sky.

Then, seemingly from out of nowhere, appeared sea gulls —the same sort of birds that had seen me off from San Francisco now forming a welcoming committee for an island I hadn't the slightest desire to visit.

At the sight of the gulls, I instantly dumped my garbage overboard. This I thought to be a fine idea. I was not only feeding the gulls but also rising up high enough to clear the island by a wide margin, to get away as far as possible from this unwelcome sight of land. However, it didn't work out quite the way I had hoped. The gulls plunged avidly into the water after my food. One of them grabbed the remains of a carcass of smoked turkey I had been living on for most of the week, took it onto the very top of my balloon, and settled down to devour it in comfort. The other

gulls, after having dived for all of the smaller pieces of food
in the ocean, flew back up to where I was and noticed their
comrade comfortably feasting on cold turkey on the top of
my balloon. This instantly set off a loud symphony of cawing, and a big fight over the carcass started to shape up at
once. This was all out of my reach and all I could do was
pace around my small porch, praying that nothing would
happen to my balloon. I leaned over the balustrade, looked
up, and saw one lone sea gull gliding very slowly over the
Globe, his head hanging down with that frightening look of
a hawk studying his prey. This was horrible. I hadn't
thought of bringing a gun with me. The gull circled slowly
around the balloon once, then dove. He plummeted

straight for the turkey carcass. Whether he got it or not, I'll never know. There was loud and confused sea gull action on top of my balloon. It seemed to me they all flew away at once—and then I heard something ghastly: the sound of a sea gull beating his wings and cawing for breath in the rarefied atmosphere inside the silken bag of my balloon.

On this seventh day of my trip, which was supposed to last a year, I found myself with a hole in my balloon the size of a sea gull.

I was heartbroken. It was impossible for me to get at the hole in order to attempt to mend it. The *Globe* had already begun to lose altitude. I had only one choice: to try to land on the island. I saw immediately that at the rate I was descending I would be in the ocean long before I reached the island. I started throwing things overboard to make my basket house lighter so that I would fly above water longer. I had no idea of the nature of the island I was approaching, so at first I decided to save all of my food in case I needed it to live on when I landed. I threw chairs, table, books, water-distilling apparatus, water cans, dishes, garbage containers, cups, saucers, charts, globes, coat hangers, clothes—everything noneatable. Clocks, scissors, towels, combs, brushes, soaps, everything I could lay my hands on I threw out through the doors, off the porch, out of the windows, the fastest possible way I could rid myself of anything which weighed anything. The *Globe* continued to descend at a speed which was far too great if I were to

55

The Unwelcome Passenger

make the island. I had to throw away my food. I threw all of the heavier canned goods first. This wasn't good enough. I threw the fruits, vegetables, smoked meats, everything in my house. I looked overboard. I was but a few hundred feet above water and the island was still over a mile off. Then I discovered something new and worse in the way of horrors. A school of sharks was following me in the water beneath and swallowing the food I threw as soon as it hit the water. This meant that I had to make the island or fall among the sharks. I was desperate.

The Twenty-One Balloons

There was nothing left in the house to throw overboard.
I emptied my pockets, saving only my pocket knife. I threw
the clothes I was wearing next, all of them except my right
shoe. I walked around the porch and, clinging to the window sills with my arms, I kicked the balustrade and uprights off the porch with my right foot. The balloon still
had a half mile to go. There was only one thing left to do.
I climbed up on the roof of my basket house, pulled the
ladder up and threw that overboard. With my pocket
knife, I cut four of the ropes which attached the house to
the balloon—one from each corner—and tied them se-
curely together. I looped my left arm through these ropes.
I then grabbed my knife and slashed all of the other ropes

supporting my house. My basket house fell and splashed among the sharks and the *Globe* gave a small leap upward. I dropped my pocket knife, kicked off my right shoe, and prayed.

A minute or two later, I felt my toes hit the water and I shut my eyes, afraid to look and see if any sharks were about. But my toes only skipped once or twice on the water's surface when I found myself being dragged across the beach of the island and the giant deflated bag of the *Globe* came to rest on top of a tall palm tree.

I was exhausted, burned by the sand, and too weak to crawl out of the sun into the shade. I must have gone to sleep on this beach.

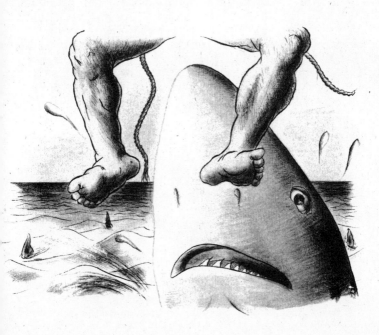

V

A New Citizen of Krakatoa

FTER HAVING SLEPT FOR WHAT MUST HAVE been four or five hours, I found myself being gently awakened. I opened my eyes. My body was bright red from sun and sandburn. I looked up at what I thought was a man kneeling over me, shaking my shoulder and saying in perfect English, "Wake up, man, you've got to get some things on and get out of the sun, wake up, wake up." I thought that this must be part of some delirious dream. The idea of a man who spoke English on a small volcanic island in the Pacific seemed so odd. I shut my eyes again. But as soon as I did this, I felt my shoulder again being shaken and heard this same voice which kept saying, "Wake up, wake up; you've got to get in the shade!"

I shook my head and opened my eyes again. There was a man kneeling over me. As I sat up he stood up. He was handing me some clothes, and he was dressed in a most unusual manner. This man wasn't a native, and didn't suggest an explorer or a traveler. He looked like an overdressed aristocrat, sort of a misplaced boulevardier, lost on this seemingly desolate volcanic island. He was wearing a correctly tailored white morning suit—if you can imagine such a suit—with pin-stripe pants, white ascot tie, and a white cork bowler. The suit he was urging me to put on was just the same as the one he had on, only in my size.

"Am I dead?" I asked. "Is this Heaven?"

"No, my good man," he answered, "this isn't Heaven. This is the Pacific Island of Krakatoa."

(When Professor Sherman mentioned the word "Krakatoa," a shudder of excitement ran through the audience. Only recently there had been news stories telling that half of Krakatoa had blown up in the greatest volcanic eruption of all times.)

"But I always thought Krakatoa was uninhabited," I told the gentleman in the white morning suit as I started painfully to put on the clothes he was handing me. "I always heard that the volcanic mountain made living on the Island impossible."

"This is Krakatoa, all right," he said. "And we who live here are most pleased that the rest of the world is still convinced that Krakatoa is uninhabited. Hurry up, put on your clothes."

I had put on the white pin-stripe trousers and the shirt as the gentleman handed them to me. The shirt had starched cuffs, a small white starched dickey, and a detachable wing collar. I didn't bother putting on the collar, and started rolling up my sleeves. "Let's go, lead on," I said.

"Come, come," said the gentleman from Krakatoa. "You can't come and visit us like that. Is that the way you would call on respectable people in San Francisco, New York, London, or Paris? Roll down those sleeves. Put on this collar, vest, and coat." As he was saying this he was smiling warmly to show that he meant no ill feeling but was merely setting me straight on Krakatoa style and manners. "I'll admit," he continued, "that on other islands in the Pacific it is considered quite the thing to give up shaving, forego haircuts, and wear whatever battered white ducks and soft shirts are available. Here, we prefer a more elegant mode of life. You, sir," he said, "are our first visitor. I am quite certain that you will be rather impressed with the way we live and with the various aspects of our Island. I hope you will be impressed anyhow, for since we believe in keeping this place absolutely secret, I believe you will be finding yourself spending the rest of your life as our guest."

While he was talking, I had obediently rolled down my sleeves. He handed me a pair of cuff links made simply of four diamonds the size of lima beans. He handed me diamond studs with which to do up my shirt front. I attached my wing collar. He held a small mirror so that I might more easily tie my white ascot. As I donned my white bowler I was filled with many emotions. I thought that this was without doubt the most extravagantly absurd situation in which I had ever found myself. I was also giving a large amount of thought to that remark of his about being a guest of the people of Krakatoa for life. It was with deep, mixed feelings that I assured the gentleman that I was already quite impressed.

"Well, come then," he said. "First I'll show you our mountain."

He led me through a small forest of palm trees. The underbrush was thick and wild, quite similar to the untouched jungle life found on any Pacific island. My host walked through this in a most peculiar way. He was holding up his pantlegs and gingerly picking the right spots on which to rest his feet so as not to disturb the creases in his suit. My suit being a borrowed one, I felt that I had to treat it with equal care. We must have made a funny sight: two gentlemen in white suits and white bowlers tiptoeing through the jungle.

A New Citizen of Krakatoa

Suddenly a remarkable change took place in our surroundings. As we neared the mountain, the underbrush in the jungle became less and less bothersome and then ceased to exist altogether. Instead of thick wild roots, giant ferns, banyan trees, and the usual webs of jungle vegetation, I found myself walking on soft green grass which smelled and looked as though it had just been mowed. It had evidently been given all of the care of a lawn on an English estate. It was like a tropical garden in the zoo of some great Capital. I was quite astounded by this and remarked about it to my host. He explained that the underbrush had been cleared everywhere except for a fringe of jungle all the way around the Island. This made the Island seem uninhabited to passing ships.

When we were about a hundred yards from the foot of the mountain we stopped and sat on a bench. I took the opportunity to introduce myself. "My name is Professor William Waterman Sherman," I said, extending my hand. He shook hands with me and said, "I am Mr. F."

"Mr. F. what?" I asked.

"Simply Mr. F.," he said. "I shall have to explain about that later. The reason I suggested that we sit down on this bench is that we are quite close to the mountain. The mountain has been quiet all morning. This is rare. It is seldom quiet for more than an hour at a time. When the mountain starts rumbling, you will feel the whole island move violently beneath you. You will find this to be quite frightening and disagreeable at first. We all did. It will take

you some time to get what we call 'mountain legs.'
'Mountain legs' are to us what 'sea legs' are to sailors.
Many of us were sick, in the same manner as a passenger
gets seasick on a rough voyage, when the mountain used
to rumble before we got our 'mountain legs.' I am just
warning you of this phenomenon so that you won't be
scared. The land is roughest near the mountain."

As if this explanation had been a cue for the mountain
to perform, we had no sooner left the bench and continued
on than we heard a noise like muffled thunder coming
seemingly from underfoot. This noise became louder and
louder, and the surface of the earth started to shake and
roll. I ran back to the bench, lay on it, and clung to it with
all my might. I looked at Mr. F. He was watching me,
smiling amiably, and was calmly moving up and down
with the surface of the earth like a bottle in rough water.

A New Citizen of Krakatoa

The earth didn't crack or split beneath us at all. I thought at the time that being in Krakatoa was like riding on the back of some giant prehistoric animal. The noise could be compared to great abdominal rumblings. The surface of the earth was like some huge bit of hide, stretching and buckling over monstrous muscles and bones.

Mr. F. waved to me to come on. He was standing in a very casual way as if on firm ground except, of course, that he was moving up and down. I felt positively drunk. I fell down four times between the bench and Mr. F. To my complete shame and disgust, I became violently ill while attempting to rejoin my companion. Mr. F. helped me off the ground. He grabbed me by the arm with a firm grip as though he were escorting some drunk away from a lawn party.

"You can see now why Krakatoa was always considered unfit to live on," said Mr. F.

"I couldn't be more completely convinced," I groaned.

"That's the peculiar thing about nature," explained Mr. F., "it guards its rarest treasures with greatest care. Every year on other Pacific islands hundreds of natives lose their lives trying to bring up pearls from the floor of the sea. Man pays nature dearly for pearls. This noisy volcano on Krakatoa has frightened men away from the island for centuries. This fickle, dangerous, and fearful mountain has a mine at its feet. I am now leading you to this mine."

With considerable difficulty, due altogether to my stupid inability to walk as easily as Mr. F., we reached the foot of

the mountain. We were suddenly standing on a piece of
ground which didn't move at all. I can assure you that I
was considerably relieved. There was another bench on
this motionless piece of earth and I ran to it and sat down.
I looked out over the quivering landscape and listened to
the thunderous rumblings. I found I couldn't stand even
to look at it for any length of time, for just the sight of this
billowing lawn and the bending and bobbing palm trees
almost made me ill again. Mr. F. sat beside me for a while
and then suggested that we move on. He took me to a wall
of the mountain behind this second bench. There appeared
to be an entrance in this wall, an entrance covered up by an
old wooden door from a ship. Mr. F. reached in his pocket
and took out two pairs of glasses with dark lenses. "You'll
need these," he explained, "and whatever you do, do not
remove them while in the mines." I put them on. Mr. F.

moved the old door to one side and asked me to follow him. I obeyed.

As soon as I entered the mines I understood why the ground above, where I had just been, didn't move. I understood why the walls about me didn't move, why the ceiling and ground beneath me didn't budge, and why this was a peaceful retreat in a rumbling, throbbing landscape.

Ladies and gentlemen, the walls, the floor, the ceiling of this mine were hewn out of the hardest of all of nature's minerals: pure, clear, dazzling diamond. I was up to my ankles in diamond pebbles. The floor was covered with diamond boulders and diamonds as big as cobblestones. If the famous Jonkers' diamond had been tossed on the brilliant floor of the Krakatoa diamond mines, it would have been as impossible to find as a grain of salt in a bag of sugar. This was diamond in its cleanest state, ready to be cut; pure crystallized carbon unblemished by any form of dirt or impurities.

I was naturally dumbfounded. I had read about and seen pictures of the famous salt mines of Poland, the crystal caves of Bermuda. Here was a sight a thousand times more blinding, infinitely more awe inspiring; a sight to make reality of the most imaginative fairy tale.

I waded around in the diamonds, picked up great handfuls of the jewels letting the smaller ones slip through my fingers. I juggled with two heavy diamonds the size of baseballs. I suddenly felt like a small child let loose in a candy shop.

"May I have some of these?" I asked. My voice was trembling.

"Sure," he said, "fill your pockets if you wish. But come outside with me for a moment."

I eagerly stuffed my pockets and followed him out of the mine. The light in the sun outside seemed dark in comparison with the sparkling, blazing, spangled brightness inside the mine. Even without our dark glasses it seemed as though the blue sky had suddenly turned gray. It was hard at first to distinguish any color in the tropical landscape. But then our eyes became used to the comparative darkness of sunlight and the grass again became green, the sky blue, and my companion's complexion took on a healthier glow.

"Sit down," he said, pointing to the bench nearest the mine. "I have quite a bit to tell you. You may think that your landing on this island was all by accident. The only accident is that the wind blew you exactly in the direction of Krakatoa. The fact that a hungry sea gull dove into your balloon, forcing you to land here, might be termed an accident; but if that hadn't happened, I would have made several holes in your balloon with this pistol. So in any case you would have landed here, sooner or later, unless a shift in the wind had suddenly blown you off in a different direction. If you had flown over Krakatoa, you would have been the first outsider ever to do so; you would have seen that there are houses on the island, you would have seen our buildings, parks, and playgrounds. You would have told the rest of the world that there are people on Krakatoa. We wouldn't have liked that at all. A young boy, the son of Mr. B., sighted you early this morning; and I was sent to the beach with a pistol to make sure that you landed here. I was chosen because I am one of the better hunters on the island. You have seen our diamond mines, that is, you have seen one of them; there are many other unexplored plots of ground around the base of the mountain where the earth doesn't ever move. Do you understand now why you will have to remain our permanent guest?"

"I do indeed," I assured him.

"Later on, after you have had time to think this all over carefully, I am convinced that you won't have any desire to leave Krakatoa at all. There is fabulous wealth and power attached to owning a share in the mines. You do own a share now, because the ownership of the mines is divided equally among all who know that they exist. We might have killed you when you landed here, and kept the secret from you in that violent way. We are fortunate here in that there are no murderers amongst us.

"So now that you are here, you are automatically a citizen of Krakatoa. You own a share of the mines. If you could possibly spend the amount of money you are worth at the present cost of diamonds in other countries, you would have to spend a billion dollars a day for the rest of your life. But if you took your share of diamonds, loaded them in a freighter, and carried them with you to another country you would be making a horrible mistake. Diamonds are priced as high as they are because they are extremely rare jewels in other countries. Unloading a boatload of diamonds in any other port of the world would cause the diamond market to crash; the price of diamonds would drop to next to nothing; and your cargo would scarcely be worth more than a shipload of broken glass.

"Every year, the men of Krakatoa take trips to some foreign country in the world, a different country every time. I shall tell you about these trips in detail later. We buy our supplies for the year and return to Krakatoa. We each take with us one fairly small diamond which we sell to different brokers in different big cities of the country we visit. At first we thought it necessary to solemnly swear that we wouldn't tell anybody of the whereabouts of Krakatoa, the secrets of our diamond mines. But this wasn't at all necessary. You will find that out as soon as you go to a different country. You'll start thinking of the fabulous wealth in diamonds you have back in Krakatoa, realize the power of diamonds in other countries, and remember that telling of Krakatoa would destroy the diamond market. You will find out that you will avoid even mention of the Pacific Ocean. Your only fear will be that you will talk in your sleep.

"You asked me a short while ago if you might have a few diamonds. Help yourself. It is only natural to want to carry some around your first few days here. We are so used to them that we just leave them in the mines. They are worthless to us here. We each own a fortune about one hundred times as big as the Treasury of the United States, but there is no place here to spend money, so we leave them where they are."

This talk made me feel rather silly. I sheepishly walked to the mines and tossed back the paltry half-million dollars' worth of stones I had picked up. My mind was in a turmoil. The excitement of my crash, the rolling of the ground, these unbelievable mines had completely exhausted me physically.

The earth had stopped rolling by this time for one of its brief few daily pauses. Mr. F. pointed to an extraordinary group of houses in the distance. "That is our village," he explained. "We are headed that way."

Fearing that the earth would again start to pitch and roll, I ran to the village from bench to bench. I was followed closely by Mr. F., who seemed to take great enjoyment in my fear of the volcanic action of the earth. When we at last stopped in front of Mr. F.'s house, I was completely worn out.

"Will you lead me directly to my room?" I asked him. "I feel I have had quite enough excitement for today. After a good night's sleep, I know that I shall be in far better condition to cope with the novelty of this fabulous Island."

Mr. F. kindly showed me to a room, gave me some pajamas, brought me a meal, and said, "Good night."

I thanked him, ate the meal in bed, and shortly afterward dropped off into heavy slumber.

COAT OF ARMS OF KRAKATOA

Diamond-shaped emblem in tropical setting representing frying pan heated over volcano, symbolic of the Island's *Gourmet Government*. Motto: *"Non Nova, sed Nove"* — "Not New Things, but New Ways."

VI

The Gourmet Government

I WOKE UP THE NEXT MORNING AFTER A NIGHT of peaceful and heavy sleep. I knew I had slept well and in complete comfort because I am a great dreamer; and when all is well at night I dream pleasant dreams. On uncomfortable nights, I have nightmares. That night I dreamt I was back on my inflated mattress in the *Globe*. You can well imagine my surprise when I woke up in a big and beautiful antique canopied bed in an exquisite bedroom, furnished in Louis the Fourteenth style. The wallpaper of my room was pale blue with gold fleurs-de-lis. The curtains were red velvet, each trimmed with a large gold cloth sunburst, symbolizing the opulence and extravagance of the "Sun King," Louis the Fourteenth of France. I hadn't noticed the room at all the night before. While eating my supper in bed by the light of one candle, I had seen that I was in a canopied bed; but I suppose that my mind, in an effort to put my body at ease, tired as I was by the excitement of the day, had pictured the room as the sort of simple American Colonial bedroom I had become so used to at home.

I got up and put on my clothes. I found that someone

had taken away the slightly wrinkled suit I had worn but
a few hours the day before, and replaced it with a complete
fresh one. This was quite to my liking. As I was dressing, I
heard a knock at my door and Mr. F. walked in. We

exchanged greetings and I assured him that I had spent a most comfortable night. While we were talking, I heard the sinister rumbling noise coming from the direction of the mountain. I went to the window, looked out, and saw that the ground below had started to move again. It didn't go up and down with the violence it had the day before near the mountain, but rather looked like animated furrows in a plowed field. Mr. F. explained that the ground didn't move much in the village which was situated as far as possible from the mountain. I asked him why it was that the house we were in didn't move when the earth did. His answer was extraordinary:

"The Bible tells us to build our houses on foundations of stone," he said; "on Krakatoa we have found it necessary to use an even stronger foundation. Our houses are built on a substructure of solid diamond boulders. Come," he added, "I'll take you out to breakfast."

On my way downstairs, I noticed that Mr. F.'s house wasn't consistently Louis Fourteenth in style, but was furnished in the best French tastes of many different periods. I saw other rooms, some Louis Fifteenth, some Empire.

As I left the house I turned around to take a look at its outside appearance. The building was the same as the Petit Trianon in Versailles, a building which I have always considered one of my favorite pieces of architecture. This was all an unbelievable dream—to think of finding such a building on a small island in the Pacific.

I looked around at other buildings. They were equally fabulous. As I stumbled along the rippling ground I noticed, in this order: a replica of George Washington's Mount Vernon house; a typical British cottage with a thick thatched roof; a lovely Chinese pagoda; a building of typical Dutch architecture; a small copy of Shepheard's Hotel in Cairo; Mr. F.'s French house; and about a dozen other houses all representing different nations. We were heading for the British cottage. We entered the cottage, walked into the dining room where some eighty other people were eating breakfast. As we walked in, Mr. F. announced in a loud, clear voice, "Ladies and Gentlemen, may I present Professor Sherman, the new citizen of Krakatoa." I was given a most cordial welcome. Everyone in the room stood up and applauded; then the men came toward me, their hands extended. I was introduced in order to a Mr. A., a Mr. B., a Mr. C., right on through to a Mr. T. The man named Mr. B. was evidently my host at this British cottage. He led us to a table. We sat down. I immediately turned to my companion and said, "Mr. F., before I become any more confused, if such a thing is possible, will you please start from the beginning and tell me the history of Krakatoa? Will you please tell me how all of these lovely people got here? Will you please explain why each house is entirely different in architecture, why the two houses I have visited so far both have gigantic dining rooms? Will you please tell me why all of the men here have the names of the letters of the alphabet? I have never thought there could be a country in the world so foreign and confusing as to customs as this one appears to be."

Mr. F. laughed. "First of all, let's get some breakfast," he said. We went to a huge table where in large silver chafing dishes could be found large quantities of the deliciously prepared kidneys, mutton chops, and bacon which make up the hearty British breakfasts. We helped ourselves and returned to our table and Mr. F. told me the story of Krakatoa:

"Eight years ago, a young sailor now known as Mr. M. was shipwrecked off the Island of Krakatoa in a tremendous hurricane. He landed on the Island in good physical condition, which was extremely fortunate for him because the rest of the crew of the ship he was on were drowned in the Ocean. As soon as he felt the earth rumbling beneath his feet, he knew he was on that most dreaded of islands, Krakatoa. He didn't want to go near the mountain, for he knew that the volcanic action of the mountain caused all of that violent shaking in the earth. He couldn't stay on the beach, though, because the winds of the hurricane caused a blinding and extremely dangerous sandstorm which would destroy any man. He instinctively made his way for the shelter of the jungle. He crawled through the jungle toward the mountain, trying to get as far away from the beach as he possibly could. He must have had a horrible time of it, for he was not only being thrashed by the bending trees and wind-whipped underbrush of the jungle, but was also going up and down with the sickening motion of

Krakatoa's surface. Sometime during the night he crawled up on that peaceful plot of ground near the mines where the earth doesn't move. He groped around in the dark looking for shelter and finally found a hole in the wall of the mountain which he thought to be a cave. He crawled in and slept in comparative peace but in great discomfort. He woke up, of course, in the diamond mines.

"His first thoughts, upon suddenly discovering that he was the richest man in the world, were naturally of how to get off Krakatoa and back to civilization with a sizable load of diamonds. At that time, getting off Krakatoa was a difficult thing to do. It is hard to leave a place no outsider dares to approach. This was a good thing in a way, because it gave him a chance to get used to living on Krakatoa, to realize that one could live on Krakatoa, and to think out carefully the best way of taking full advantage of the enormous wealth attached to the mines.

"He built himself a raft which took him a month to complete because at first he didn't have any tools. He found a diamond in the mines the shape of an axe head and made an axe of this. It was a crude tool, but one which never needed to be sharpened. He finished the raft and set out to sea one afternoon when he sighted a ship in the distance. He took with him only four diamonds, three small ones about the size of marbles and one large one about the size of a baseball. The ship picked him up. It was headed for the United States. He told the Captain of the ship that he had been shipwrecked on Krakatoa, invented horrible

stories about how terrible the place was to live on. The Captain, however, needed no convincing, for he had no desire whatsoever to go to Krakatoa.

"When Mr. M. arrived in San Francisco, he sold the three smaller diamonds to three different diamond brokers for approximately ten thousand dollars apiece. Then he picked twenty families, the twenty families you see here; and using the huge diamond the size of a baseball as bait, lured them into taking a trip with him back to this fabulous Island. He picked the families with care. Each family was required to have two things in order to be chosen. They had to have: a) one boy and one girl between the ages of three and eight; and b) they had to have definite creative interests, such as interests in painting, writing, the sciences, music, architecture, medicine. These two requirements would not only assure future generations of Krakatoa citizens; but also he assumed that people with creative interests are not liable to be too bored on a small desolate island; and people with inventive interests can more easily cope with unusual situations and form a stronger foundation for a cultured heredity.

"With the thirty thousand dollars Mr. M. made by selling the small diamonds, he bought himself a ship. Mr. M. was the only man of the selected families chosen who was a sailor. He proceeded to make sailors out of all the other men by carefully training them on cruises on the ship he had bought. We were soon a capable crew. We loaded the ship with our families and supplies, and sailed away. That was about seven years ago.

"Krakatoa is situated between Java and Sumatra. It is in a small group of three supposedly uninhabited islands named Krakatoa, Verlaten, and Lang. Verlaten Island hides a small inlet of Krakatoa from possible sight from Sumatra and also protects the inlet from the rough sea. We planned to dock our ship in this inlet. We did this in the middle of the night.

"Our first year on Krakatoa was pretty horrible. Upon seeing the mines, we all became rather piggish. There was no way of actually dividing the diamonds except by making twenty shares, that is twenty pieces of paper each entitling its owner to an equal part of the mines. A greedy desire seemed to be in each of us at that time to become the one and only owner of all of the diamonds. Some of the families were made up of architects and builders. They built themselves comfortable little huts and settled down to a rather normal way of living. We were sleeping either on the ground or in the shelter of the mines. We asked the builders to make us houses too. They agreed to do it only if we gave them our shares in the mines. We refused at first, then found out (after months of uncomfortable living in the height of the rainy season) that we all simply had to have huts. We gave our diamond shares to the four building families. They made us our huts in return for which they became the owners of the diamond mines.

"Now that we all had houses, we all started thinking of ways of getting our diamonds back. There was nothing to buy on Krakatoa. We lived mostly off the abundant vegetation on the Island. The climate is humid, warm, and steady; the earth, due to its volcanic nature, is full of phosphoric acids and potassium, and everything grows well here. One of the families opened a restaurant. This was an excellent idea. The four families who owned all the diamonds were anxious to show their power. There was no way of spending their diamonds here. There was no way of getting to another country either, except in our ship. It took all of the men on the Island to make up the ship's crew, and none of the families without diamonds had any desire to take the families with diamonds back to the United States. So the families with diamonds showed their power by "eating out" every night at the restaurant. The restaurant owners charged a fabulous price for their meals; I

think it was three meals to the share. In spite of this the restaurant idea seemed to work. Soon another family opened a restaurant which was just a little better, and then another house was turned into a restaurant, and after a while every house was turned into a restaurant and the diamonds started to become equally divided again. After about four months of fierce competition in which we all became excellent cooks, we found that we each had our shares back and that we were all considerably happier. There was a tremendous variety of cooking to be had from house to house, and we decided to celebrate the regaining of our shares with a big banquet in which each family would contribute its favorite dish. It was a sumptuous affair and we ended it by drawing up a Constitution for the Government of Krakatoa.

The Gourmet Government

"We have an unusual Constitution. It's sort of a Restaurant Government. There are twenty families on the Island, each running a restaurant. We made it a law here that every family shall go to a different restaurant every night of the month, around the village square in rotation. In this way no family of Krakatoa has to work more than once every twenty days, and every family is assured a great variety of food."

I understood now why the two houses I had visited were both apparently restaurants, so I asked Mr. F. to explain to me how the families got their alphabetic names.

"That's quite simple," said Mr. F. "There are twenty restaurants around the village square here. We lettered them, A, B, C, D, E, and F, all around the square up to T, the twentieth house. We changed our names. In "A" Restaurant live Mr. A., his wife Mrs. A., their son A-1, and their daughter A-2. In "B" Restaurant live Mr. B., Mrs. B., B-1, and B-2; it's very simple."

"Is there anything else unusual in your Constitution?"

"We have a different calendar in Krakatoa. It too is a Restaurant Calendar. The months are shorter. There are twenty days to the Krakatoan month, and they are named after the families, 'A' Day, 'B' Day, 'C' Day, and so forth up to 'T' Day. There are eighteen months to the Krakatoan year. Each day of one of our months, we eat at a different restaurant. On 'A' Day, we eat at the A.'s Restaurant, on 'B' Day at the B.'s, and so forth. Each family only has to work on his day of the month."

"That's reasonable," I remarked. "But tell me, how did each restaurant get to be so different? You have told me that all of the families come from San Francisco. From what I can see and hear of them they all seem to be Americans, yet their houses are as varied and international as the pavilions at a World's Fair."

"We are all Americans here. The international restaurants were built simply to give variety to our days. When, in the early stages of our lives here, we found that we could all live happily under the Restaurant Government, we decided to make each restaurant different so that on certain days we could look forward to having a food which was unusual and good to eat. We Americans all have different inherited tastes so we decided that each restaurant should serve the food of a different nation. We arranged this alphabetically also. The A.'s run an American restaurant and serve only real American cooking. You are now eating at the B.'s. This is a British chop house. The C.'s run a Chinese restaurant. The D.'s run a Dutch restaurant, the E.'s an Egyptian restaurant; you can run through the alphabet up to T. The T.'s run a Turkish coffee house."

"And you, Mr. F., run a French restaurant?"

"It's as easy as that," said Mr. F.

"Is there a Krakatoan restaurant?" I asked.

"Naturally. It is run by Mr. K. and specializes in dishes of strictly native foods; odd dishes prepared from the bread of the bread trees, the milk from the trunks of the milk palms; cocoanuts, bananas and more exotic fruits

and mostly the wonderful fish which are so easily found in the ocean which surrounds us. We couldn't think of what style of architecture to use for a Krakatoan restaurant, so we invented one. It is made out of crystal glass bricks, to suggest the diamond mines which are the Island's most guarded treasures; and inside most of these glass bricks we have sealed rare and colorful tropical fish, because for many months they were our main source of food.

It looks like a house made of ice cubes and fresh fish and is a very inviting place to eat on 'K' Day of the hot summer months."

"What sort of restaurant do the S.'s run?" I asked.

"A Swedish Smorgasbord restaurant."

"And R.?"

"He runs a Russian tearoom."

"What a wonderful place this Island is!" I exclaimed. "I am certainly looking forward to 'I' Day, because I love spaghetti."

"Mr. I.'s Italian restaurant serves the best," assured Mr. F.

"Have you names for the months of the year?"

"We do in a way, but the names of the months are very seasonal and depend entirely on the stocks of food we have on hand. We now have a surplus of lamb, so we voted to call this the Month of Lamb. Each restaurant has been asked to serve a lamb specialty on its menu. Today is 'B' Day of the Month of Lamb, so we are having British mutton chops. British mutton chops are hard to beat. On 'F' Day, my day, I will serve lamb chops, with béarnaise sauce, or perhaps I will serve a roast of lamb cooked with garlic. On 'T' Day the Turkish coffee house will specialize in Shishkebab, which is lamb cooked on metal skewers. Of course our restaurants serve a choice of meats, but in the Month of Lamb you can always count on one lamb dish in all the menus."

"The more I hear of Krakatoa, the more I like it

There's just one more thing which puzzles me. How do you get your supplies? How did you get all of the materials to build these houses?"

"That was a direct result of the Restaurant form of government. We are all so happy here that none of us has any desire to give away the secrets of Krakatoa's diamond mines. We have given up fighting between ourselves for selfish control of the mines, so we have nothing to keep us from taking frequent trips to foreign countries. We always go to different countries. We cover up our trail by frequently selling our freighter and buying a new one. No boat of ours has ever been seen in two different countries. By simply picking up a handful of diamonds from the floor of our mines we are able to make enough money in foreign countries to fill a new freighter each trip with the best of everything we need. The last of our houses was completed recently. They have taken seven years to build. It has been a long and gradual process on which we have all worked very hard."

"How about me?" I asked. "I have just arrived here. I have no family. Do you want me to change my name? Should I start building myself a restaurant? I hate to think that I am in any way upsetting anything here. Another restaurant would ruin your calendar. What do you want me to do?"

"I am afraid," said Mr. F., "that you will have to be in the peculiar but rather happy position of being a perpetual guest. You may stay in my house as long as you want, or

THE F. FAMILY

move around if you wish. As for the food situation, you will simply follow our daily calendar and eat with us every day. When a family prepares for eighty people, it isn't at all bothered by an extra guest. As for changing your name, I wouldn't advise it at all. Since you won't have a restaurant there will be no need to name a day after you. Another good reason is that the twenty-first letter in the alphabet is 'U.' You wouldn't want to be called Mr. U. Everytime somebody said, 'Hey, you!' you would have to turn around. If someone asked you who you are, you would have to answer, 'I am 'U.' You would keep overhearing snatches of conversation which would bother you If someone were to tell a friend, 'I want to see you tonight,' you would wonder what was meant by 'you.' You would keep asking yourself, 'Does "you" in this case mean "you" or "U"? If "you" means "U" and "U" is me, then that lady wants to see me tonight.' And then you would wonder why. I tell you, Professor Sherman, 'U' is a bad name."

I laughed at this and agreed with Mr. F. to leave my name alone. Then Mr. F. told me that he had a most unusual house to show me. "It's the house of Mr. M. who runs the Moroccan restaurant. He not only discovered Krakatoa but he has also discovered ways of making life more pleasant. Mrs. M. is a nurse. The children, M-1 and M-2, have very inventive minds. Come with me and I'll show you what I believe to be the most fantastic house in the world."

VII

The Moroccan House of Marvels

ON OUR WAY TO MR. M.'S HOUSE I ASKED
Mr. F. what the citizens of Krakatoa did with
all of their spare time. "You have told me that
only families with creative interests were
chosen by Mr. M. to come here. You said that people with
inventive minds were selected because they would be less
apt to be bored on a small island such as this. Well," I
asked, "how is it working out? You have nineteen days
out of each of your months in which, according to your
Constitution, you have no work to do—are you bored, or
have you interests here which keep you busy?"

"We are kept busy here in much the same manner as
people are kept busy in any other country, except of course
that the diamond mines which we own place our living on
a slightly higher standard. Keeping busy in other countries
is usually interpreted as earning a living. Earning a living
means in its simplest form providing food and shelter. Our
Restaurant Government takes care of our food needs. We
have devoted our combined creative abilities to making
our shelters as magnificent as possible. We built the houses
which you see now one at a time. We chose a house for

95

each represented country which we thought was most typically beautiful of that country, and then went ahead and built it. For instance, my house is very much like the famous Petit Trianon. I bought the detailed plans of the Petit Trianon in a little shop in Versailles. We had the stones all cut to order in France and loaded them in our ship, and brought them back to Krakatoa. These stones were all numbered and lettered, corresponding to the plans. Building my house was as enjoyable to us as a huge set of toy blocks is to a young child. On subsequent trips we bought suitable furniture. We all worked together until each house was completed. The builders supervised the actual construction; the painters either selected paintings, made copies of originals, or made paintings of their own for the houses. We handled, furnished, and decorated each house as a hobby; the fabulous hobby of the richest families in the world—which is what we happen to be. It has kept us working pretty hard."

"Is the food here always good?" I asked. "Or do some families, either out of laziness or lack of interest, prepare poor meals on their days?"

"No one seems to have slipped up yet. As soon as you start to run a restaurant you become tremendously interested in food. I suppose that it is simply pride which makes one try to make better meals than the other families. You see, on your day every family comes to your house to eat. I always find on 'F' Day that I am somehow trying to prove that my day is best. Then there is this to consider we are all interested in food and look forward to eating. If I were to prepare a poor 'F' Day at my house, I would have reason to fear that the others would do the same on their days and we would have a miserable month of food."

"I understand," I said.

"But then everything doesn't work out as neatly as I have made it seem, particularly now that our houses are all finished. To be sure, we work very hard on our day of the month; but recently we have spent considerable time in doing absolutely nothing at all."

"What's wrong with that?" I hastily asked.

"Nothing!" shouted Mr. F. "I am happy to see that you are a good loafer. Certain prudish people in other countries seem to find that 'busy hands are kept out of mischief,' or some other such silly idea. We have developed loafing on this Island to such an expert extent that even our hands are completely relaxed. Our only work now, besides cooking, is in trying to make life more pleasant for ourselves and for each other. The house you are about to see is one on which we have all been working lately. It was one of the first to be completed and now we are going all over it with new improvements. If some of our inventions work in this house we will install them in our own houses.

"From the outside," continued Mr. F., "you can plainly see that Mr. M.'s Moroccan house is of simple and solid construction. That is one of the main reasons why we chose it to work on first. It is easier to adapt new ideas to a house of simple rigid lines than it would be, for example, to a

house with domes and minarets and towers such as Mr.
T.'s Turkish coffee house. We discovered right away that
almost all of us had ideas of improvements that required
some form of mechanical motive power, so we first of all
made over the cellar of Mr. M.'s house. The usual cellars
of our houses are filled with barrels of wine. We dug a separate cellar next door, lined it with the usual diamond
boulders to make it sound and immovable, built a roof
over it, and moved Mr. M.'s fine Moroccan wines into this
new private cache.

"Most of our ideas required hydraulic pumps to put
them in motion, so we first installed a steam engine in Mr.
M.'s cellar—but here we are. Come, I'll take you first to
the cellar."

We were greeted at the door by Mr. and Mrs. M. and
their children, M-1 and M-2. They hadn't had so many
things to talk about at breakfast and had reached their
home long before we had. Mr. M. sensed immediately that
Mr. F. was taking me on a tour of inspection of his house,
so rather than complicate matters he said that his house
was ours for the morning and to feel free to wander through
it and inspect it as we liked. "I'll go downstairs and get
some steam up," he said, "in case you feel like trying out
any of the inventions."

We followed Mr. M. down into the cellar. There was a
boiler and furnace which looked to me much like the
equipment to be found in the cellar of any American home
and Mr. M. told us that stoking the fire for a steam engine

was no more difficult than keeping an ordinary furnace running. The room was well insulated because on a tropical island it would be impossible to live in a house heated by the sun above, and a furnace below. Of course the boiler was piped to the pistons of a huge steam engine—this was different from anything found in the ordinary American home. The rest of the cellar was an extraordinary maze of polished brass shafts running from the floor to the ceiling. The flywheel of the steam engine furnished power to operate numerous hydraulic pumps which evidently made these brass shafts go up and down. The steam engine was also attached to an electric generator. This whole cellar was sort of a mechanical jungle more complicated than the engine room of a ship. I was anxious to get

out of there fast, first of all because I was dying to see what all of this machinery operated upstairs; and then too there seemed little space in this huge room in which to move around without being burned, smeared with grease, crushed, or receiving electric shocks. Mr. F. seemed to feel the same way about the room, and only Mr. M. and м-1 and м-2 felt at home as they dashed about through this brass forest checking dials and gauges.

I noticed, as we were about to leave, that two long white sheets of cloth were coming from a slit in the ceiling down into the cellar. These wide cloth bands passed through a sort of large flat boiler, then on through what appeared to be the kind of drying machines used in paper factories, then back through rollers up another slit in the ceiling.

"What in the world is that?" I asked.

"Come," said Mr. F. "First I shall show you Mr. and Mrs. M.'s bedroom."

We walked upstairs and into a bedroom on the first floor. It was furnished in excellent Moroccan taste. I say excellent with some reservations. I personally am not too fond of that style. But aside from these observations, I noticed nothing unusual about the room at first.

"Have there been improvements made in this room?" I asked.

"Mrs. M. used to be a nurse," replied Mr. F., "and to nurses bedmaking seems to become extremely boring after awhile. If you stop to think of it, nurses in large hospitals spend a good deal of their time in making beds. It is natural that they should soon tire of it, particularly when they suddenly find themselves to be as rich as Mrs. M. We all came to Mrs. M.'s rescue with this amazing bed. It has continuous sheets."

"How does it work?" I immediately inquired.

Mr. F. walked over to Mrs. M.'s bureau, opened the top drawer, and took from there a crank. He inserted the crank into a hole in the footboard of the bed and asked me to watch closely. He started to twist the crank and the sheets started to move across the bed, passing on rollers through a sideboard on through the floor. "When I twist this crank," explained Mr. F., "the sheets pass through this

sideboard down through the floor into the cellar. There, they pass through a boiler where they are washed, then through a drying machine. They next pass through steam-heated rollers where they are pressed; then come up through the floor, through the other sideboard of the bed on rollers, and back to the top of the bed. This continuous sheet is marked off in bed-widths. Every morning Mrs. M. simply turns the crank until a bed-width has passed from one side to the other side of her bed. This action starts the washing machines, diverts heat from the furnace to the drying machine, and while one length of sheets is being pressed, fresh widths of hot white sheets are revealed on her bed."

"Incredible!" I exclaimed. "But what about blankets?"

"Good Lord, man," said Mr. F., "we never use blankets here. We're just a few miles below the Equator."

"Oh, that's right," I said. "Have you made inventions for every room in this house?"

"We have. Each family originally chose a room to work on, although several families have worked on some rooms. We were all interested in the dining room. I'll show that to you next. You see, there are many problems attached to feeding eighty people, even if it's only once a month. There are four members to each family, and the children help a lot; but even so you can well imagine that the problems of preparing an elaborate breakfast, clearing that off and preparing a lunch, getting that out of the way and getting dinner ready are big and tiresome. What do you think of this dining room?" he asked.

The Moroccan House of Marvels

I looked at the room we had just entered. It was enormous but absolutely bare. The floor was highly polished and had sort of a design of disks on it, one large disk surrounded by four smaller ones. This design was repeated twenty times on the floor. The walls had pictures hanging on them, scenes of charging Arabs on horseback and portraits of marabouts, sultans, and viziers.

"It looks more like a Moroccan ballroom of some sort," I answered. "Where are the chairs and tables?"

"Exactly," said Mr. F. "It's easy to clean, eh, Professor Sherman? No tables to sweep under, no chairs to get in your way."

"Perfect," I answered. "But what do you eat on?"

At this a wild look came over Mr. F.'s face. "Watch this," he said. He walked out in the hall and pulled a great lever. He came back to my side and took me over to the far corner of the room. "Look at the floor," he said. I looked. There were suddenly small wisps and puffs of steam coming from the circular disks on the floor, then these disks started to rise slowly like some nightmarish garden of mushrooms, and soon each group of disks was up out of the floor forming little groups of four flat stools around little round tables.

"Cleaning up is easy here," he said. "After M-1 and M-2 have removed the dishes, silverware, and tablecloths, Mr. M. lowers the chairs and tables by pressing the lever, and Mrs. M. and he then wash the floor. Chairs, tables, and floors are all taken care of for the month in one motion."

William Pène du Bois

"*Bravo!* What goes on in the other rooms of this Moroccan house of marvels?"

"The livingroom isn't by any means perfected," he said, "but I'll show it to you if you want to see it."

"Lead on."

"You see," explained Mr. F., lowering his voice considerably, "Mr. P., Mr. Q., and Mr. R. were poor but extremely inventive scientists when they were picked by Mr. M. to come to Krakatoa. They are all three of them fascinated with the extraordinary power and many uses of the electric current. It was they who insisted that the electric generator be attached to the already heavily burdened steam engine in the cellar. I think all of their new-found wealth has gone a little to their heads. Mr. M. wasn't awfully anxious to turn over his livingroom to them. He feels that their ideas are perhaps a little too advanced, even for Krakatoa. But what could he do? He had already given a room to each of the other families to work on, so he felt obliged to turn over the livingroom to these three remaining inventors."

"What in the world did they do to it?"

"Electrified all of the chairs and the couch," said Mr. F. in the hushed whisper of a man who is describing the work of a maniac.

"*What for?*" I exclaimed hastily as I was about to enter the livingroom.

"They say that it's to move around the room more easily. I'll show you how they work."

I wasn't too anxious to walk into this electric livingroom, but felt that it was safe to follow Mr. F. wherever he went. The floor was made of steel. The chairs all had a decidedly unusual look about them. First of all, on the left arm of the chairs (they were all armchairs) there was a little tiller much like the tiller of a sailboat. The chairs were on little wheels. There was a rod up the back of these chairs with sort of a steel brush on the end of it which touched the ceiling. The ceiling was covered with a wire mesh.

"The scientists who 'improved' this room say that man spends too much effort moving his chair around the room or walking from his chair to the window, bookcase, or table to get his pipe and so forth. They figured out that some men walk an unnecessary half mile a day, just around the livingroom. These chairs are supposed to save people this trouble. Look," he said. He sat down in an armchair and drew the tiller around in front of him. "I shall now move effortlessly around the card table and stop in front of the window. There is a button at the end of this tiller which I will press to start me off. I will steer the chair with the tiller, and stop it by taking my thumb off the button. Are you ready?"

"Go ahead," I said, backing into a corner.

Mr. F. pushed the button in the tip of the tiller. The chair shot around the table at breakneck speed, stopped in front of the window with such suddenness that Mr. F. was plunged head first out of the chair out through the open window. A shower of blue sparks followed the trail of the chair as the brush rubbed on the mesh ceiling.

"There," said Mr. F., climbing back through the window out of breath and with a most distressed look on his face. "You can see that this is hardly what one might call an improvement in livingrooms."

"Why don't they slow them down a bit?" I asked.

"The scientists who designed these infernal machines insist that they could slow them down. But Mr. and Mrs. M. have had so many sad experiences, such as shocks and

bumps, in the room that they refuse to have electric chairs
of any sort. M-1 and M-2 are crazy about them, however.
The room has been turned over to them and their play-
room has been made into a livingroom for Mr. and Mrs.
M. All of the children on the Island spend many hours a
day driving the easy chairs around the room, yelling and
screaming and bumping into each other. The couch holds
about four children and is the fastest in the room. I would
hate to predict what will become of this younger, mechan-
ically minded generation."

I agreed that the electrical age we were entering was indeed frightening.

William Pène du Bois

"What are the bedrooms belonging to M-1 and M-2 like?"
I asked. "Are they furnished with beds with continuous
sheets too?"

"No," said Mr. F. "After seeing the chairs and tables
we installed in the dining room, they designed beds of their
own. Their beds have levers on them and move up and
down. Their rooms have skylights, like the upstairs rooms
in most Moroccan houses. They can move their beds up
to the ceiling and look through the skylights at the stars;
or they can open the skylights and move right up on the
roof on hot nights. A little over the height of the roof is as
far up as they go. On the other hand, they can lower their

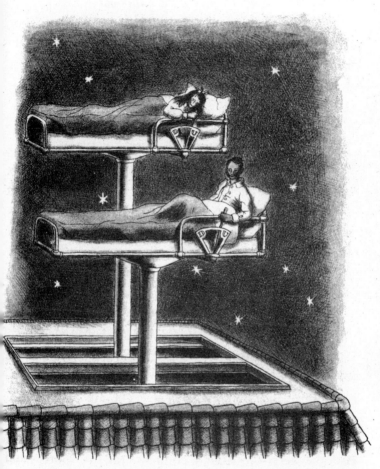

beds right through the floor of their bedrooms into their bathrooms below. We are having a hard time deciding what sort of bed we are going to install in our own houses: the bed with the continuous sheets of Mr. and Mrs. M. or the elevator bed of M-1 and M-2. Both models have many fine features, you will have to agree.

"The other rooms in the house have improvements too, such as walls divided into decorated revolving panels which permit a complete change of décor at the press of a button; kitchens with dish washing and drying machines—the whole house has every imaginable convenience, we believe. I have shown you all of its most spectacular aspects."

"It leaves me speechless," I muttered. But then as I started thinking it all over, I suddenly exclaimed in a very loud voice: "I'm a balloonist, and I must admit this kind of efficiency rather bores me. For instance, I far prefer your stunning and elaborately elegant Hall of Mirrors dining room to the mechanized mushroom grove we have just visited. It seems strange to me that mechanical progress always seems to leave the slower demands of elegance far behind. With all of the peace and spare time on this lovely Island, why should any part of your lives be speeded up?"

"Many of us are in complete agreement with you," said Mr. F. "The artists all are. The scientists express themselves through a different medium. You are a balloonist. If you are interested I will show you the two remaining innovations we have made on this Island. One of them, our Balloon Merry-Go-Round, combines the two sports most dependent on Nature, ballooning and sailing, and should please you immensely. On the success of the other invention the lives of the families of Krakatoa depend. I saw your balloon, the *Globe*, and I know that you are a balloonist of great ingenuity. I am sure you will like these two balloon inventions."

The Moroccan House of Marvels

"Ladies and Gentlemen," announced Professor William Waterman Sherman, "before telling you of the two balloon inventions of Krakatoa, I am going to call a fifteen-minute intermission. This will give you a chance to digest the many inventions I have already discussed, and it will give me a few moments of rest. The end of my story is, I suppose, the most exciting part of it; for as you know from having read your newspapers during the last month, the time is near at hand in this account for the lovely Island of Krakatoa to start blowing up. Thank you very much for having been such an excellent audience up to this time. Come back in fifteen minutes and I'll tell you of two extraordinary inventions and of one history-making explosion. Thank you."

The audience spent three of their fifteen minutes applauding and cheering and then went outside for a stretch and a breath of fresh air. Professor Sherman poured himself a glass of water, drank it, stretched out on his bed, looked up at the ceiling, and prepared to spend a most comfortable and relaxed intermission.

VIII

Airy-Go-Round

URING THE INTERMISSION, THE MAYOR and the Chief Surgeon of the San Francisco General Hospital rushed to Professor Sherman's bedside to see if he was all right. "Are you tired?" they asked in one voice. "Would you rather resume tomorrow?" asked the Mayor. "How do you feel?" asked the Chief Surgeon. "Is there anything we can do for you?"

"I feel fine," said Professor Sherman.

"Would you like one of the nurses to change the drinking water in your carafe?" asked the Chief Surgeon.

"I don't care, it tastes all right to me."

"Could I fetch you a little refreshment?" asked the Mayor. "Something to renew your strength."

"If you insist," said the Professor. The Mayor ran off at a fast puffing trot while the Chief Surgeon busied himself tucking in the comforter on the Professor's bed. It should have been obvious to anyone, even two such important personages as the Mayor and Chief Surgeon, that all Professor Sherman wanted during this intermission he had called was a few minutes of rest.

The Mayor came back with a nip and the Professor swallowed it in one gulp. Then, looking at the Mayor and Surgeon, he said with a smile on his face, "You know, Gentlemen, this to me is very funny. A little over a month ago, I was an insignificant arithmetic teacher who would have found it almost impossible to get to see either one of you. Now you are waiting on me like a pair of well-trained valets. I thank you for your kind attention. It goes to show how wonderful ballooning can be. You never can tell where the winds will blow you, what fantastic good fortune they can lead you to. *Long live balloons!*" he shouted. The Mayor and the Chief Surgeon joined in with a few sheepish giggles, then backed away.

By this time the fifteen minutes were up and Professor Sherman was gratified to see that the people of the audience had quietly returned to their seats and were sitting attentively. The packed auditorium wasn't making a sound. It was waiting anxiously to hear the end of his extraordinary story.

The Chief Surgeon saw, as before, that the Professor was comfortably propped up with pillows, and the Mayor walked over to the Professor's bedside. With one hand resting on the head of the bed, he turned to the audience and said:

"Again it gives me great pleasure to present Professor William Waterman Sherman."

The Professor thanked the Mayor, cleared his throat and resumed his talk:

Airy-Go-Round

Mr. F. led me to the first invention he had promised to show me, the Balloon Merry-Go-Round. On our way I told Mr. F. that the name of the invention suggested something at an amusement park. "Just what is this invention for?"

"It is part of an amusement park," said Mr. F., "which the children of Krakatoa are planning for themselves. You see, our children now are between the ages of ten and fifteen. When we return from our trips to other countries, they help us unload our freighter with great interest. It suddenly dawned on them a year or so ago that it would be an excellent idea if a few boatloads were brought back full of supplies exclusively for them; for after all they do own a share in the mines, too. We agreed to give them two boatloads a year, so all of the children held a meeting to decide how best to fill their freighters. This amusement park they have started to build is the result of their planning. The Balloon Merry-Go-Round is their own invention, designed with but little help from us."

"Is there any school here?" I asked.

"The children have no formal schooling. We have taught them how to read and write, and we have tried to teach them a little arithmetic. They have all taken part in the building of our international houses—which is most educating in itself. But all in all, a school is sorely needed here. You aren't by any chance a teacher, are you? Just what does the title Professor stand for in your case?"

"Professor of, uh, Aeronautics," I stuttered. "I teach Balloon Theory at, uh, the San Francisco Lighter than Air

School." I felt a flush of heat in my cheeks as I waded through this fabulous lie. I had no intention of getting involved again in teaching, the very thing from which this trip of mine was intended to take me.

"How interesting," said Mr. F. "That goes to show how quickly one gets out of touch with one's native city. I can't say that I even recall hearing of such an institution."

"It's one of the latest," I muttered, "practically brand-new." Then quickly changing the subject, I asked what other forms of amusement could be found at the park.

"So far, they have just had time to design and build the Merry-Go-Round, but they have a lot more planned. Most of the usual rides found at amusement parks are impractical for Krakatoa because they are higher than the jungle life on the Island and would be visible from the sea. As a matter of fact, we only take rides on the Balloon Merry-Go-Round after thoroughly scanning the horizon for passing ships. We never use it if anything is in sight. Do you see that tall pole in the distance?"

"Yes, I do," I said. The pole was straight and the same width at the bottom as at the top. It was threaded like a gigantic screw and it was about seventy-five feet tall.

"That's part of the Balloon Merry-Go-Round, the axle around which it revolves to give it its spin when it is gaining altitude."

"Can't that be seen from the ocean?" I asked.

"Yes, it can. But one lone pole isn't enough to attract much attention from passing ships."

116

Airy-Go-Round

We came to a little forest of palm trees, the same sort of neatly kept little forest I had seen the day before, with freshly cut lawn instead of the usual jungle underbrush. We walked through this forest for a hundred yards or so and then came upon a clearing. In the middle of this clearing was what was apparently the Balloon Merry-Go-Round. There were eight little boats around the base of the pole, all joined together bow to stern. In the place of oarlocks, there were two brass rings on these boats, and through these rings passed poles which all met at the main vertical pole of the Merry-Go-Round where they were screwed into the hub of another large brass ring around the pole, forming spokes of a giant wheel. Each boat was covered with a protective tarpaulin. Mr. F. removed one of the tarpaulins and showed me one. They were nice little centerboard sailboats, sturdy and quite seaworthy. The sails were neatly stowed in trim lockers. I didn't notice any masts, but there was definitely a place for them. Alongside of each of these boats was a large deflated balloon painted a pale sky-blue. Off to one side in the clearing there was a little shack made of bamboo which reminded me very much of my basket house. On its walls outside, eight silk hoses were hanging, neatly coiled up and in line. There was a bell on top of this little shack, which could be reached by climbing a ladder.

Mr. F. walked over to the shack, went inside, and came out again with a spyglass. He climbed up the ladder to the roof of the shack and carefully looked over the horizon around him, apparently for ships. "Would you care to risk a trip in it?" he asked me. "The weather today is ideal."

"As an ardent balloonist, I accept with enthusiasm; but as a sixty-six-year-old man I must confess that I accept with some trepidation. Is it safe?"

"Absolutely," answered Mr. F. "You don't believe that we would allow our children to make ascensions in dangerous contraptions, do you?"

"I guess not," I said, reassured. "I am sure that any invention using balloons and wind as motive power cannot but be enjoyable."

"Very well, then," said Mr. F. He then loudly rang the bell on top of the shack. This sound produced the same reaction, only considerably happier and more excited, as a school bell back home. We were shortly surrounded by children. These children didn't seem to need to be explained anything either; as soon as they arrived in the clearing they made themselves extremely busy readying the Balloon Merry-Go-Round. They took the tarpaulins off all the boats and rolled them up neatly. Four of the children ran into the shack where they prepared the hydrogen machine and pumps. Another eight each grabbed a silk hose, attached it to the hydrogen machine in the shack on one end, and to one of the balloons on the other. The balloons were all carefully unfolded and laid out flat on the ground, and the nets and ropes which attached them to the boats were carefully placed around and beside them so that they wouldn't get tangled up when the balloons were filled with gas. Slowly the balloons started to fill with hydrogen.

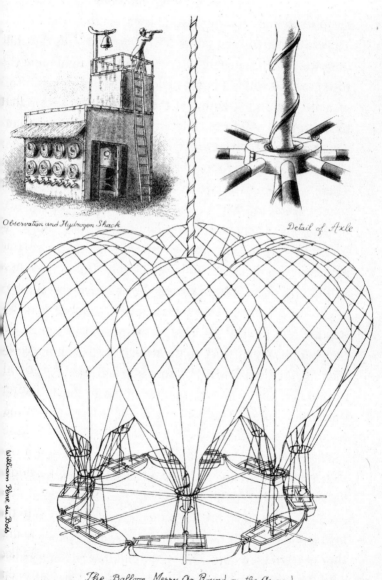

Observation and Hydrogen Shack

Detail of Axle

William Pène du Bois

The Balloon Merry Go Round on the Ground

the ones nearest the pumps filling faster than the others. They lazily lifted themselves off the ground with the children watching them carefully, constantly straightening the ropes so they wouldn't get tangled. Soon they were all full of hydrogen and straining at the boats which were roped to the ground. All forty children were present, working efficiently on the Merry-Go-Round, although it was apparent that there was only room for fourteen of them on this trip. There was room for two in each boat, making a total of sixteen seats, but Mr. F. and I were going to occupy two of the seats. There was no arguing among the children as to whose turn it was; they must have had some sort of passenger schedule they followed closely. I did notice that neither B-1 nor B-2 were among the children who climbed into the boats when they were ready. I suppose that this was because it was "B" Day of the Month of Lamb and they had plenty of work to do at their British chop house. I sat in a boat with Mr. F.'s son, F-1, and Mr. F. sat with a child in a boat which was on the opposite side of the big pole from ours. "This will make the Merry-Go-Round balance better," said F-1.

There were two children on the ground near each boat. When we were all aboard, they detached the silk hydrogen hoses and rolled them back up to the shack where they carefully hung them up. They then returned to us and one held a rope at the bow of each boat and the other held a rope at the boat's stern. One of the children passengers had a blank pistol, the sort used for starting races at track meets. He stood up and yelled in a high clear voice, "*Is everybody ready?*"

A shrill and deafening "*yes*" was heard, mixed with the deeper voices of Mr. F. and myself. At this signal, the children standing near the boats all gave their ropes a sharp pull, which seemed to unhook the boats from the ground, and they all ran around the pole in the direction we were heading, giving us a good fast start.

The boats were joined together to form the rim of a wheel. The poles going through the brass oarlocks of the boats formed the spokes of this wheel. The spokes were attached to a big brass ring, or hub of the wheel, and this whole gigantic Merry-Go-Round revolved around the seventy-five-foot pole which was pointing straight up to the sky and was threaded like a screw. The balloons lifted the boats around and around the huge screw up into the air. The Balloon Merry-Go-Round gained speed as it gained altitude. The pole was well greased so that by the time we neared the top we were going very fast. I asked F-1 what happened when we reached the top of the pole. "Do we quickly deflate the balloons and revolve back down to the ground around the pole in the opposite direction?"

"Of course not," said F-1. "We fly right off the pole into the air."

"How do we keep the wheel straight when it's in the air?"

"You'll see," he said.

We soon reached the top and the Merry-Go-Round

121

lunged upward as it lost its grip on the pole. The wind immediately started to carry us off over the Island. We were gaining altitude fast and, of course, still spinning around at great speed. I must admit this was a truly delightful and exciting ride, unlike any other balloon experience I have ever had. I saw now how the boats were kept level. A child in each boat held the ripcord of his boat's balloon. Whenever a boat went a little higher than the others, the ripcord would be pulled releasing a little hydrogen until the boat was again on the same level.

"You must only be able to take short trips," I told F-1, "if you constantly have to release gas to keep the Merry-Go-Round level."

"That's right," he answered. "The length of our trips depends on many things such as the calmness of the weather, how well we distribute the weight in the boats, and how skillfully we control the ripcords. But you understand," he added, "the Balloon Merry-Go-Round wasn't built for travel but rather for short pleasure trips."

"Oh, of course," I said.

The Balloon Merry-Go-Round was heading directly for the mountain. I saw that we were going to fly over it. I asked F-1 if this were not dangerous.

"It isn't dangerous, but it's rather unfortunate because it always means a short trip."

"Why?" I asked.

"Because the huge crater of the volcanic mountain is full of hot air which forms sort of a vacuum. When we fly over

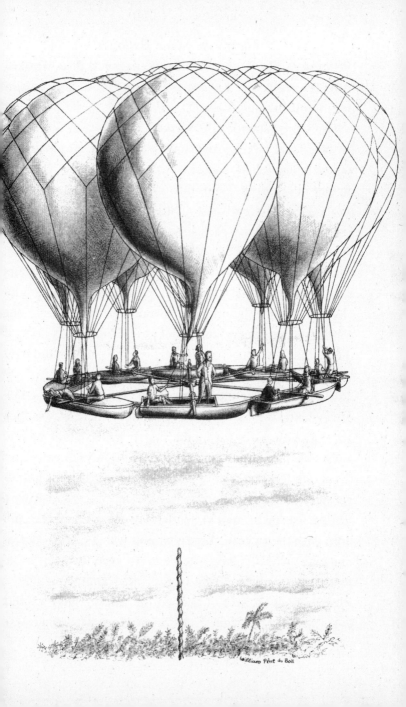

William Pène du Bois

the crater, the Merry-Go-Round is sucked downward rather violently and we always use up a lot of gas controlling it and keeping it level."

"Isn't this hazardous?" I asked.

"No," said F-1, "by the time we reach the mountain, we will be high enough to clear it by a great distance. The only danger in taking a ride in this is landing on the ground or on the mountain, or worst of all, in the mountain when the wind is calm. Krakatoa is a small island, and if there is any wind at all, it will carry the Merry-Go-Round out to sea. Once when we first got it, we took a trip on a very calm day. We went straight up, spun around a while, and gradually lost altitude, landing in a forest of palm trees. No one was hurt, but some of the boats were damaged and one of the balloons was torn. Since then, we have only risked trips when there is wind."

We were nearing the mountain and I leaned over the side of my boat to look down at the crater. There was a thick gray smoke crawling around inside. It was like looking into a horrible pit full of elephants. When we were directly over the mountain there was a sickening atmosphere of hot air permeated with sulphurous gases. The Merry-Go-Round started tossing around violently over the pit, and the children with the ripcords kept a careful watch directly across our giant wheel at opposite boats to keep the Merry-Go-Round as steady and level as possible. Hanging on tightly, I leaned over the side of the boat in order to have a direct look into the volcanic crater itself. In places where the

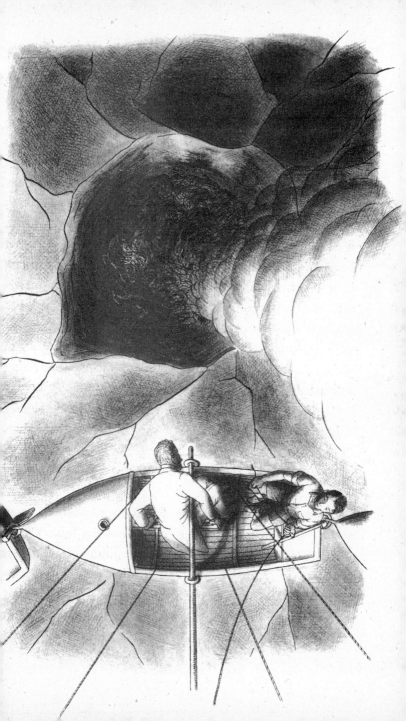

smoke had cleared a bit I could see a lake of thick molten lava boiling and bubbling in slow motion. It was a sickening, frightening sight. As I was leaning over, the Merry-Go-Round suddenly plunged downward, then swayed from side to side as the children steadied it. I must have taken a deep gasp of breath, out of fear, I suppose, and my lungs were suddenly filled with hot sulphurous fumes. The Merry-Go-Round was still spinning fast, as well as pitching and rocking in the air. I hastily drew my head back into the boat, shut my eyes, and lay down on the bottom of the boat. I could hear the rumbling of the mountain beneath me mixed with the hissing noise of hydrogen being released from the balloons. I think I was as close to being sick then as it is possible for anyone to be. We were soon over the mountain and in fresh, calm air again and I sat up feeling considerably better.

"To tell you the truth, Sir," said F-1, who apparently could well see that I had nearly lost my British breakfast, "I was nearly sick myself that time. The mountain seems unusually violent this morning. I hope this isn't a bad sign."

I took this to be the remark of a younger balloonist comforting an older one who had nearly made a fool of himself. I told him that my behavior was quite inexcusable.

Flying over water in this spinning airship was completely enjoyable. The magnificent seascape of the Pacific Ocean passed before your eyes half of the time, and Krakatoa in its entirety was beneath you for your careful observation with each turn of the Merry-Go-Round. The Island looked beautiful from the air. Its vegetation was so rich, warm, and soft-looking. The mountain looked so fearful and exciting. The magnificent houses of all nations looked like extraordinary doll's houses on felt lawns, and the Krakatoan crystal house shone like a jewel. The contrast between the trimmed interior and untrimmed ring of jungle around the Island was easy to see from our boats. The Island looked like a formal garden surrounded by a bushy untrimmed hedge.

After a flight lasting approximately thirty-five minutes we were near the surface of the water. The children, controlling their ripcords like experts, lowered the Merry-Go-Round gently and smoothly into the Ocean. We made one complete turn in the water and came slowly to a stop. "Well," I exclaimed, "that was undoubtedly the most thrilling and unusual trip I have ever had the pleasure of taking."

The children in the boats, Mr. F., and I then all leaned back and relaxed a while in the sun, looking up at the balloons which were now half empty and bobbing back and forth with the wind. Suddenly one of the boys, the same one who had fired the starting gun, stood up and said, "All right, everybody, let's go."

At this command, the rest of the children stood up and carefully deflated their balloons and folded them up in their boats without letting any part of them touch water. They folded them lengthwise first, then rolled them from

127

the top toward the bottom where the gas escape was, thus forcing all of the gas out of them and making small neat bundles. They opened the little lockers in the boats, where the sails were, took the sails out, and replaced them with the folded balloons. Each boat had one mainsail.

"How do you sail these boats when they are all attached together like a wheel?" I asked. "And what do you use for masts?" These were foolish questions, I immediately realized, for while I was asking them I managed to figure out these problems for myself.

First of all, the children detached the boats one from the other at their bows and sterns. When this was done, they were still attached to each other by the poles which formed the spokes of the giant wheel. These poles were obviously the masts when the boats were used for sailing. The children, two on each pole, all pushed together toward the center hub until the poles slid out through the brass oarlock rings on their boats. Then, still working two on each pole, they unscrewed the poles from the brass hub in the center. They all unscrewed their poles except one boy, the boy who gave the commands. He pulled his pole in with the hub still attached to it, unscrewed the hub in his boat, and put it away in a separate locker. Now that they each had their masts, it was a simple problem to put them into the mast holes. Mr. F. and I did our best to work as efficiently as any of the other crew members. Soon the mainsail was rigged up and we were ready to sail back to the Island. Only the need for a boom was absent from this com-

pact invention. We lowered the centerboards and lined up. It was evidently the custom to race home. The boy who gave the signals took out his gun, fired it, and we were homeward bound as fast as the wind would take us. I am afraid I was more of a hindrance than a capable assistant to young F-1. We finished the race last by about seven minutes. The boats were moored to a dock near the freighter in the hidden inlet and we assembled on shore. F-1 explained to me that the boy who had given the signals was the "Captain of the Day," some sort of honor each child received in turn.

The Captain of the Day told the rest of us that since this was my first trip in the Balloon Merry-Go-Round, the results of the boat race wouldn't count on the Official Scoring Sheet. F-1 let out a whooping cheer at this which made me feel quite badly. The Captain of the Day then took me aside and told me, in a most polite way, that he thought it would be an excellent idea if I learned a bit about sailing since I now found myself to be a citizen of Krakatoa. I assured him that I would.

The Captain of the Day then closed the meeting by saying that the Merry-Go-Round would be reassembled around the flying pole right after supper. "And I want you all to be here and help," he said, looking sternly in my direction.

After forty years of schoolteaching I found myself being ordered about by a child. I couldn't help but find this heretofore impossible turnabout amusing. I was indeed far away from the usual dull school routines I so disliked.

"*I'll be there!*" I said in a loud voice, as everybody looked at me and laughed.

The whole trip had taken about five hours and we had therefore missed lunch. I devoured an excellent supper at the B.'s chop house, and then Mr. F. and I reported to the flying pole. The Captain of the Day rang the bell on top of the shack assembling all of the children and we were divided into eight groups of five. (B-1 and B-2 were still busy.) With five on each boat, we had the Merry-Go-Round reassembled and ready to go in less than half an hour. I will confess, though, that after this busy second day on the fabulous Island, I was well ready for bed and slept like a top.

William Pène du Bois

IX

Concerning the Giant Balloon
Life Raft

THE NEXT MORNING I ATE BREAKFAST WITH my fellow-Krakatoans at Mr. C.'s Chinese restaurant. I will tell you quite frankly that I have no idea of what I ate at any of the meals on "C" Day. I am not too partial to Oriental food and didn't even dare to ask what I was eating for fear that any accurate description or analysis would only add to the uneasiness with which I suffered through each meal. I noticed that many of the children toyed with their dishes with equal apprehension. I used their method of eating some of the portions which consisted of removing the toasted almonds from the top carefully, with a fork, and leaving the rest. Mr. F. scolded me for this display of timidity and poor taste, and told me that to acquire an appreciation of good food I should show a little more courage and will to experiment. I assured him that I had a great desire to become an accomplished gourmet while living under the Restaurant Government, but preferred to arrive at this in gradual stages over a long period of time.

Mr. F. asked me what I wanted to do after breakfast. I told him that being on the Island in the position of a perpetual guest with no work to do, I was fast getting to think of living in terms of holidays back home. On a hot Sunday in San Francisco like this "C" Day of the Month of Lamb in Krakatoa, I would most probably go to some beach and do some swimming. I suggested a swim to Mr. F. He thought this to be a fine idea so we put on bathing suits and bathrobes and made our way through the outer fringe of jungle to a nicely cleared fine coral beach. I had arrived in Krakatoa on the afternoon of "A" Day. It was now the morning of "C" Day. In that short time, I had become quite used to walking about on the moving landscape. I was amazed at how fast I had acquired my "mountain legs" and felt rather proud of myself.

The little beach looked very funny to me when I stopped and thought about it and compared it to beaches back home, for here the ocean was quite calm and the beach was going up and down.

"How's the swimming here?" I asked.

"Excellent," said Mr. F. "You'll see."

I waded in the water up to my waist and there experienced a delightful sensation. The sand beneath me rose up with the surface of the earth until I found my feet out of water. It then lowered me down in the water up to my neck. I stood in one place and went in and out of water, spending a few seconds in the blazing tropical sun and then being dunked again up to my neck in clear cool water; up and down, in and out, without having to move at all from the place where I was standing. Mr. F. had waded out a little deeper in the water than I had and seemed to enjoy being entirely dunked up over his head at the earth's lowest drop, and then rising with the earth until he was only up to his knees in water. Once when temporarily up to my waist I dove in toward deeper water to do a little swimming. I hadn't gone very far when I felt the sand rise beneath me and lift me by the stomach out of water, a most peculiar feeling. Mr. F. explained to me that it was necessary to wade out quite far to do good swimming. "You should walk out far enough so that you are up to your waist in water when the surface of the earth beneath you is at its highest rising point." I did this, half walking and half "dog paddling," and when I was far enough out, enjoyed a good swim.

Back on the beach Mr. F. and I decided to take a sun bath. He told me that he had found it best to let the surface of the earth roll you around when it moved and not to try and lie in any one position. We did this and were nicely toasted on all sides by the hot sun. I was enjoying a most pleasant morning and decided right away to make this a daily habit.

The night before, I had borrowed an atlas from Mr. F. and had looked up Krakatoa in it before going to sleep. I found that it was situated in the Sunda Strait between Sumatra and Java and that it was about twenty-five miles from both of these two huge islands. Looking at the map and trying to trace the path of my voyage in the *Globe*, I was amazed to see how much land I had missed on my trip. I must have flown between Mindanao at the southern end of the Philippines and the Celebes Islands over the Celebes Sea. I must have flown over Borneo one whole night, narrowly missing mountains and being at times very close to the ground. I shuddered when I tried to imagine the rude awakening I would have had if the *Globe* had struck a mountaintop in Borneo while I was peacefully asleep on my inflated mattress. The Pacific Ocean is the biggest body of water in the world. Krakatoa, which was only eighteen square miles in size, was one of the smallest Islands in the Pacific. I set out to land in Asia, the world's biggest continent, completely missed many enormous islands, traveled thousands of miles over water, and landed on this tiny piece of land. Had a sea captain set out across the Pacific Ocean for, let us say, China and missed it by a few thousand miles and landed instead on Krakatoa, he would have been stripped of his commission and had his ship taken away from him. But to balloonists, stories such as mine are typical, and balloon trips are only considered unusual if you arrive within one hundred miles or so of your planned destination. I was thinking how delightful this all was, of the freedom and surprise of balloon travel, and of the Balloon Merry-Go-Round I had taken such a fantastic trip on that afternoon. Then it occurred to me that the Balloon Merry-Go-Round was a pretty big affair, and it seemed to me that it should be visible, when up in the air on a clear

138

day, from either Java or Sumatra. I asked Mr. F. about this while we were basking in the sun.

"We don't worry much about that," he said; "there are several reasons why. One of them is that the Balloon Merry-Go-Round is painted sky blue and therefore isn't really visible from too great a distance. Another is that the Balloon Merry-Go-Round never goes over five or six miles on its longest trips, and that doesn't bring it very close to either Java or Sumatra. Then too, the mountain has a reputation for belching forth strange things and the whirling balloons and boats look quite like a big blue smoke ring from the distance. But there is this very important reason why we don't worry about its being seen: in 1877, our second year here, the mountain was so violent that it scared the people living on the shores of the Sunda Strait in both Java and Sumatra so much that they moved their homes inland about twenty-five miles on both islands. The whole of Krakatoa was violently rocked from end to end. Waves were formed in the Sunda Strait traveling outward from the Island as a center, giant waves which swept onto the shores of Java and Sumatra completely inundating many homes. The noise was formidable and the waves caused so much damage that the people moved away from the tips of the islands in great haste. We have reason to believe that no one dares to live within a radius of fifty miles from us."

"Great heavens!" I exclaimed. "How did such an explosion affect you who were living right here on the Island?"

"It was quite bad. Many of the huts we lived in at the

time collapsed like card houses. No one was hurt much though many of us were knocked unconscious or had our wind knocked out from being thrown abruptly to the ground. The noise of the explosion wasn't too bad on the Island. I suppose the fact that we were right on the Island made the noise more bearable. If you stand right near or on a large artillery piece when it is fired, you are much less bothered by the noise than if you are fifty feet away. We picked ourselves up, helped those who needed help, and went about the business of rebuilding our houses."

This brought up another point that had been puzzling me. "Why," I asked Mr. F., "do you people live here on top of this dormant volcano when with a handful of diamonds you could live a life of lavish ease and comfort in any other country?"

"Your question is a puzzler, and there is really no logical answer to it. It suggests a series of other questions of exactly the same nature. For instance: why doesn't a millionaire in any other country consider himself rich enough to retire, why does he try to make another million? Why do tycoons with several millions of dollars try to make a billion, a sum so huge they couldn't possibly spend it in a lifetime? As long as our diamond mines are kept secret here we, the twenty families of Krakatoa, match the rest of the world in wealth. The diamond mines have a peculiar magnetic effect on us. We couldn't live happily in any other country, we would be haunted with the unbelievable dream of this unheard of wealth back on the Island. But we can't

take our diamonds, that is all of our diamonds, to another country without destroying their value. We are slaves of our own piggishness, we have locked ourselves in a diamond prison. On the other hand, we're very happy here; and I suppose the fascination of knowing that we are each one of us richer than the combined Midases, Nabobs, and Croesi of history enters too into the Krakatoan spell which keeps us here."

"But this spell, as you call it, seems a little unreasonable to me for the simple reason that it challenges a will of human nature that is far greater than the will to be rich, this being obviously the will to live. How can you live happily here under the constant threat of being blown sky high? Now that I think of it, this whole Island is like a turkey stuffed with nitroglycerin. The surface of the earth here which is right at this moment moving us gracefully up and down is obviously activated by molten lava. A crack in the earth's surface and the cold waters of the Pacific would rush in. Imagine what would happen then, cold water coming suddenly in contact with molten lava. This hollow rumbling shell would suddenly find itself like a covered kettle of boiling water on a stove—the resulting steam would cause pressure enough to blow the top right off the whole Island. No one could survive such an explosion. What good would your diamonds do you then?"

"We're all only too much aware of this possibility. It troubles me just to hear you mention it. We have come to look upon it this way:

Concerning the Giant Balloon Life Raft

"If it should happen with the speed with which you have just described it, nobody here would have time to think or know what was happening to him. It would mean painless death. However, if we have a warning, which we all some-how expect to have, there is a quick escape from Krakatoa. Given as little time as ten minutes to get off the Island, we'll all be safe and on our way to some other country. This escape, and the fact that Krakatoa has been here an uncalculated length of time without blowing up, makes living here under the ever-present threat of extinction possible."

"What is this escape?" I asked. "Do you keep the freighter always steamed up and ready to go?"

"It would take the freighter longer than ten minutes to leave here," said Mr. F. "It's not that, it's the other invention I promised to show you yesterday. This is an invention we all worked carefully on for many months, starting right after the big explosion in 1877. Our lives depend on it, but due to its huge size and its motivating power, we are unable to try it out. There is no reason why it shouldn't work, and when I say this I mean no reason 'on paper'; its maiden voyage will have to prove its worth. It's a flying platform, a huge platform big enough to take us all swiftly into the air within ten minutes of a warning from the mountain."

"A platform capable of lifting twenty families of four?" I asked. "This makes child's play of flying carpets. How do you hope to get it off the ground?"

"With balloons," answered Mr. F.

This idea appealed to me immensely. The idea of the lives of eighty people being entrusted to such fickle and unpredictable traveling companions as balloons was quite frightening but thoroughly enjoyable.

"You are all prepared to risk your lives in a balloon contraption. I like this very much. A little while back I was starting to think of Krakatoans as being greedy, calculating, and traditionally dull billionaires. Now I find you are incurable romantics. Tell me, how can such a massive weight as that of twenty families be lifted off the ground?"

"I beg your pardon," said Mr. F., "but we are not risking our lives on any foolhardy conveyance. The balloon platform must work! It's got to work. It can't help working. Look, I'll show you."

I walked over to where Mr. F. was lying, sat down beside him, and watched him as he sketched the platform in the sand. He made a bird's-eye view of it and drew the twenty balloons around its outside edge. It was rectangular in shape. He started writing numbers in the sand. "I don't know how much the actual platform weighs by itself," he said, "it is made of the lightest pine wood in the world imported by us especially for this purpose from South America. It is made of light beams, and the floor boards are laid with spaces between them for greater lightness. The balustrade around the platform is of hollowed wood —the woodwork couldn't possibly have been made lighter. Before I tell you about the balloons I want to make it clear that I am going to give you the figures in round numbers

with the margin of error all in favor of the success of the machine; thus the lifting power of the balloons will be calculated as a little less than it actually is, and the weight we are carrying will be computed as heavier than it would actually be. There is really no accurate way of planning balloon inventions. Too much depends on atmospheric conditions, the purity of the hydrogen used, and weather conditions. I will give you the roundest of figures."

"I understand," I said.

"The balloon platform is lifted by ten large balloons of 32,400 cubic feet each; and ten balloons, half as big as the larger ones, of 16,200 cubic feet each. The larger balloons will fly higher than the smaller ones which will be situated

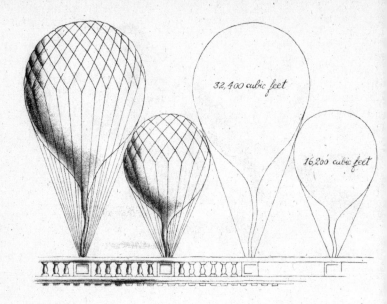

32,400 cubic feet

16,200 cubic feet

in the spaces between the larger ones thus alternating around the platform, one large, one high, and one small, one low, etc."

"I see," I said.

"The total hydrogen needed to fill all twenty is 486,000 cubic feet. Free hydrogen has a lifting power of roughly 70 pounds per thousand cubic feet. The twenty balloons have a combined lifting strength of 45,360 pounds."

"How much do you figure the eighty people will weigh?"

"Well," he said, writing down more figures in the sand, "if you divide the eighty people by sexes, half are women. If you divide them by generations, half are children. One hundred and thirty pounds per person is a safe figure under these circumstances. The eighty people will weigh 10,400 pounds. But let me see, how much do you weigh?"

146

Concerning the Giant Balloon Life Raft

"In the roundest of numbers," I answered, "I weigh 180 pounds."

"All right," said Mr. F., "that makes 10,580 pounds, leaving 34,780 pounds over to take care of the total weight of the platform."

I agreed that this all sounded very reasonable. "But one thing bothers me," I said. "How do you get the balloons filled with hydrogen and the platform off the ground in ten minutes?"

"That was our most difficult problem. Come with me, I'll show you the platform and how we think we have solved the question of a fast getaway."

I put my bathrobe on and followed him through the jungle fringe. After a good long walk, we came to a clearing which was as far away from the mountain as it was possible to get on the Island. The huge platform was situated here. I remembered having seen it from the Balloon Merry-Go-Round the day before. I had thought then, seeing it from the air, that it was some sort of outside dancing floor with a bandstand in the middle. What I thought was the bandstand turned out to be a large steel cylinder.

Mr. F. showed me four great wooden vats, one on the ground near each side of the balloon platform. There were hoses leading from the vats to the balloons in what Mr. F. described as "pitchfork connections." The hoses were large and single as they left the vats, then branched off into smaller hoses, each one attached to a balloon.

"This is how we believe we have solved the problem of a

quick takeoff," he said, "compressed hydrogen. Each of these vats contains three hundred thousand cubic feet of hydrogen compressed at sixteen hundred pounds to the square inch. The hydrogen is kept in steel cylinders which are submerged in water in the vats to keep leakage down to a minimum and keep the hot rays of the sun from direct contact with the cylinders. In the event of an emergency we will all rush to the platform, jump on, and each family will stand by a balloon. The big valves in the four vats will be turned on full force. Each family will have to see that its balloon is carefully handled so that the tremendous rush of hydrogen into it won't cause any tears, rips, or snarls. The smaller balloons will fill first. There is a lever near each balloon which controls the valve allowing gas to enter it. When the small ones are three quarters full their valves will be shut off. Shutting off the smaller balloons' valves will speed the filling of the big ones since they will be receiving all of the pressure."

148

Concerning the Giant Balloon Life Raft

Mr. F. then picked up one of the hoses and showed it to me. There was a sort of ball-and-socket connection in each hose. He explained that it took a hundred-and-fifty-pound pull to separate the hose at this connection. "Each hose has a connection such as this," he explained; "twenty hoses makes a total pull of three thousand pounds. The balloon platform isn't tied down with ropes before the takeoff, it is held down only by these hoses. Gas rushes into the balloons until the platform rises and there is a three-thousand-pound pull on the twenty hoses. The platform then tears itself away from the hose connections and leaps into the air as if it were given a huge boost. There is a valve in the ball end of each ball-and-socket connection. It allows gas to be forced into the balloon but prevents gas from escaping when the connection with the vats is broken. When the balloon platform is in the air, the hoses will be pulled in and attached to hoses from this smaller compressed hydrogen tank on the platform itself. It is with the hydrogen on the platform that flight will be controlled."

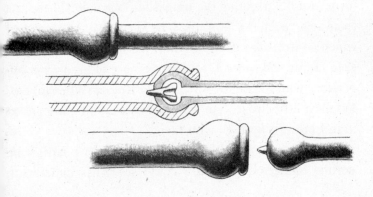

"How can you control the flight of the platform?"

"By adding hydrogen to the balloons we can go higher to a certain extent. By detaching the hoses from the tank on the platform and releasing hydrogen from the balloons, we can make the platform descend. Where we go is, as usual, left entirely to the winds. However, since we carry our own hydrogen supply, there is no reason why, with any sort of a wind and a minimum of luck, we can't travel a tremendous distance."

"How do you keep the platform level?"

"We plan to do that in much the same way as we keep the Balloon Merry-Go-Round level, only the process will be reversed. We have no desire to take long trips in the Balloon Merry-Go-Round so we keep it level by releasing hydrogen from the high side until it is even with the low side. On the balloon platform, we will add hydrogen to the low side to bring it up level with the high side so that the platform as a whole will gain altitude instead of descending. Each family will stand near its balloon on the platform, thus distributing the weight fairly evenly. There is a lever near each balloon, as I have already shown you, which controls the gas going into the balloon. The boy in each family will control the lever because of his greater experience with the Balloon Merry-Go-Round. When his balloon is a little lower than the others, he'll add more gas to it and bring it up even with them."

I walked around on the platform. The floor boards were springy underfoot and you could see grass underneath

150

through the spaces between them. I tried to imagine this huge floor in flight, looking through the boards at a city underneath. How frightening and incredible it would be, to be moving through space on such a huge piece of construction with eighty other people. The balloons were carefully folded and under tarpaulins. I took a look at several of them. They were magnificent, made of beautiful rubberized silk, and each balloon was painted many different iridescent colors. I tried to picture the reaction of people in other countries if they were suddenly to look up in the sky and see the balloon platform, its white latticed floor bordered by a graceful balustrade over which were leaning the richly clothed Krakatoans; the twenty brilliant balloons

151

above and the frightening silence with which such a huge airship would seem suddenly to make its appearance. There is no noise in balloon travel. In any other form of travel you are warned by some sort of noise of the approach of whatever the conveyance. Even ships cause a ripple of waves in the calmest of waters. Balloons are silent except on rare occasions when you might possibly hear the ghostly whistle of the wind through the ropes. There is no nicer way of traveling than in some form of lighter-than-air craft.

"The balloon platform would certainly make a delightfully attractive appearance if it should have to fly over any foreign country," I remarked.

"Its appearance played a big part in its planning," said Mr. F. "It wasn't really necessary to go to all the trouble we did in making the handsome hollow-carved wooden balustrade, or to put so much thought, work, and time into the painting of the balloons—a lighter, simpler balustrade and plain balloons would have made the platform fly just as well. If we should have to land in other countries we want to be welcomed as extraordinary visitors who have gaily announced their arrival, rather than be suspected of being invaders in some sort of aerial Trojan Horse. By the way," he added, "have you a parachute?"

"Of course not," I answered, "I threw everything overboard on the *Globe*. I didn't carry one anyway, I didn't feel I needed one."

"Each family here has a family parachute, another

invention of ours. A family parachute is so built as to keep a family of four together during a descent."

"Isn't it possible to land the balloon platform?"

"Hardly so," said Mr. F. "In the first place, it would be hard to find enough level space in which to land such a huge aircraft; and in the second place, it wouldn't be possible to deflate the balloons fast enough to prevent the wind from blowing it and dragging it across the countryside. We would have to deflate them slowly in order to make a reasonably smooth landing, and before we would be able to collapse them, the wind would drag us off, ripping the platform into splinters and endangering our lives. We wouldn't dare risk a landing in this; we plan to jump off, picking our countries and spots with care—if we ever have to take a trip on it. Professor Sherman, I would advise you to get a parachute as soon as you possibly can."

"How can I get one in Krakatoa?" I asked.

"See Mrs. M. She and her husband designed and made the family parachutes. I am sure she has enough silk left over to make you an ordinary one."

We went together to the M.'s Moroccan house and I told Mrs. M. my problem.

"Why, certainly," she said, "I can make you a parachute. But it will take me about two weeks. But then I doubt if you'll be needing it before then. I hope not anyway," she said, laughing.

"Of course not," I said. "Take your time—there's no rush at all."

X

What Goes Up Must Come Down

I SPENT THE MORNING OF AUGUST 26, 1883, or "D" Day of the Month of Lamb in Krakatoa, as I had spent the morning before, swimming and sun bathing on that delightful little fine coral beach. After having had a day of light eating at the C.'s Chinese restaurant, I attacked a Dutch breakfast at Mr. D.'s with gusto, a breakfast which included many cups of the richest, most delicious hot chocolate I have ever had the pleasure of drinking. I was afraid to go in swimming after such a huge meal, so I took a sun bath with my good friend Mr. F. for an hour or so when we reached the beach. I was pleased to see that I was getting quite tan. I got my first real burn when I made my bizarre nude arrival on Krakatoa, added to it the day we flew in the Balloon Merry-Go-Round, and considerably darkened it the morning before on the beach so that I was fast losing my comparatively pale appearance which so distinguished me at first from my fellow Krakatoans.

"Up to now," said Mr. F., as the movement of the earth's surface rolled him over near me, "you have asked me many questions which I have done my best to answer.

155

I think you now know just about all there is to know about life on the Island. Now I am going to ask you to tell me all you can think of in the way of news about my native city San Francisco, a city from which you have just arrived and which I haven't seen in over seven years."

"That's fair enough," I said. I then started to think of how best to do this. As a schoolteacher I was pretty well tied down to a rather monotonous form of urban life, but I did get to know a lot of people. I conducted classes for children between the ages of ten and fifteen, which was the ages of the children of the Krakatoan families. I reasoned therefore that the parents of the children I taught must have been the same age as Mr. F. I described San Francisco to him as a social columnist would, telling him about these people as if they were my closest friends, telling him what they were doing in terms of parties, minstrels, circuses, theaters, dinners, and whatever social functions I could remember having attended with any of them. This proved to be an excellent idea, for he had known some of the people I mentioned and had heard others talked about by friends of his on Krakatoa. I suppose one doesn't think of one's home town in terms of streets and buildings as much as one does of personal associations, friends, and relatives. Whenever I mentioned a friend of his, his eyes lit up and he started firing all sorts of questions at me. He was amazed at the many details, stories, and anecdotes I could tell about their children. "You must be very fond of children," he said; "you seem to take such a humorous and

156

sympathetic attitude toward stories of their classroom tricks and pranks." I still had no intention of telling anybody on the Island that I had been a schoolteacher but, of course, in telling Mr. F. about his friends in San Francisco, I had clearer memories of their children, to whom I was subjected every day, than of their parents, whose homes I only visited on rare and usually trying and formal occasions. "Yes," I said, gritting my teeth. "I've always been close to children."

I continued, mentioning more people Mr. F. knew and recounting as many incidents as I could recall about them. I must say Mr. F. was a good listener. He had been lying down flat on his back. He was now propped up on his elbows and seemed completely fascinated with my account. "Just a minute," he said, "I hate to interrupt you but I have a wonderful idea. Everybody here is from San Francisco and I am sure they would get the same thrill hearing of their old friends and of their friends' children as I am getting now. Would you possibly consider giving us all a talk, just like this one, in the dining room after lunch?"

"I would be only too delighted," I said.

"Wonderful," said Mr. F. "You can't imagine how much they'll like this. Our conversation here always seems eventually to get around to San Francisco and we haven't had any real news of our old friends in years."

We took a swim, let the sun dry us off, and returned to Mr. F.'s house. While I was dressing, Mr. F. ran around to all the houses preparing everybody for the talk I was going to give. I was very pleased that in this simple way I was perhaps going to be able to repay them somewhat for their fabulous hospitality.

We had a delicious lunch which consisted simply of huge portions of *Javaansche rijsttaffl* which is Javanese rice cooked and curried as the Dutch do it in the Dutch East Indies. Krakatoa is actually part of the Dutch East Indies, though no Dutchman has ever cared to set foot on the Island. We had lots of this hot rice and huge glasses of wonderful cold Javanese tea. I was pretty hot from my freshly acquired sunburn. I was warm inside from this delicious hot curry; and after several stimulating glasses of tea, I had a nice warm feeling all over and was well prepared to give my talk.

Mr. F. waited until all of the tables had been cleared by the D. family, then placed a chair on one of the tables. He silenced the crowd, introduced me as the speaker in a most informal and nice way, looked at me, and pointed to the chair. I climbed up on the table, sat down, and after the twenty families were all comfortably settled began my talk. The response to it was amazing and most gratifying. Each time I mentioned a new name, at least one face in the audience would light up. There would be much nudging of elbows, smiles, and faraway homesick looks. Giving this simple talk which seemed to bring so much genuine pleasure to these people was a tremendous joy to me. While I was talking all eyes were attentively fixed on me and I was looking around the room catching the reactions to each new name I mentioned and thinking up incidents to talk about next. Looking out of the window, I noticed that the ground seemed a little more active than usual. Being a new citizen of the Island I didn't know whether there was anything unusual about this at first. I went on with my talk. As I recall it, before being most rudely interrupted by a singularly sinister event, I had talked over three hours. I noticed that the earth was moving with increasing violence. I looked at my watch. The movement of the earth's surface usually subsided completely for a few minutes out of each hour, but that afternoon it had been getting increasingly violent over a period of two hours. This was quite alarming. I called this to the attention of the other people. They all turned and looked out of the windows. Some of them didn't seem at all alarmed but others looked quite frightened. I was far from feeling at ease. Mr. M. walked over to the window and looked out. After a few minutes he said, "I don't think it's anything to get much alarmed over. After all, most of our houses were knocked down in '77."

"But they were simple huts," said Mr. T.

"I know, but they had diamond foundations too. This house hasn't shown any signs of the slightest vibration. Please go on with your talk, Professor Sherman."

This seemed to reassure everyone considerably though I can't say my heart was in my speech as much as before. I noticed that my audience was rather restless too. *Suddenly* —and this was a sight which is as vivid to me now as it was when I first saw it—the wall opposite me slowly and almost

159

noiselessly opened up in a crack large enough to allow the sun to shine through. It was the most terrifying and sinister sight I have ever seen. A considerable amount of powdered plaster dropped on the heads of the families in the room and the windows near the cracked wall broke open. The windows had all been closed so that the usual noise of the mountain wouldn't interfere with my talk. Now, through the crack in the wall and through the broken windows, the rumblings of the mountain thundered in full force.

Mr. M. rushed to the table where I was sitting, leaped onto it, and immediately started shouting instructions. "I want all of the women and little children to run to the platform at once and start taking the covers off the balloons! I want all of the men to run quickly to their houses and grab their family parachutes (hearing the word 'parachute' at that moment came to me like a blow on the head) and dash

160

to the balloon platform! I want the six boys who are fifteen years old to take whatever food Mrs. D. has prepared for tonight and rush it to the platform!" He clapped his hands loudly and the room was emptied at once. He turned to me and said, "We've rehearsed this a thousand times; don't be alarmed, Professor Sherman, I am confident that everything will turn out all right. We'll be off in less than fifteen minutes. Now," he said, "you're the only man with no particular job at this time. We all have pretty large amounts of diamonds sewn into a pouch attached to our family parachutes. Why don't you take a bucket and see if you can get to the mines and grab some diamonds? A few big ones will take care of you quite nicely. *But don't go near the mines if it's too dangerous, please, Sherman, don't go near the mines if. . . .*" He was shouting after me, for I was off for the mines like a madman as soon as I got the gist of his suggestion. Unfortunately for me this was a waste of time. It was impossible to approach the mountain. I knew I had just a little over ten minutes time, the time needed to fill the balloons. I tried running—the action of the earth's surface threw me to the ground. I tried walking —I doddered, staggered, floundered, and tumbled. I tried crawling, but the earth's rumblings and heavings kept rolling me over on my side. I looked up at the mountain ahead and saw at once that it would be impossible to reach in the short time allotted me. I threw away my bucket, turned, and ran through the village for the platform, reeling, buckling, and falling every few feet of the way. I was the last to

161

see the Village of Krakatoa from the ground. I was there in time to see the crystal Krakatoan house splinter and flatten to the ground in a great shower of broken glass. The M.'s Moroccan house full of those amazing inventions was burning like a huge plum pudding, due no doubt to a short circuit in the electric livingroom. When I arrived at the balloon platform, it was straining at the hoses ready to leap. There were many hands extended my way. I reached up and my arms were grabbed just as the balloon platform tore itself away. I was lifted onto the platform. I remember twenty pops like champagne corks in rapid succession as the rubber ball-and-socket connections were broken, and the eighty-one Krakatoans swiftly bounded off into the air.

The first moments on the platform were bedlam. Some of the women were screaming. Some of the children were crying. The men were feverishly trying to connect the hoses to the hydrogen tank, and the boys who controlled the levers allowing gas to enter the balloons were shouting at the men to hurry up so that they could level the platform. We were flying right at the mountain on an uncomfortable slant and we weren't gaining altitude very fast. It required a certain amount of patience and a hundred-and-fifty-pound push to snap the hose connections together. The men in their frantic hurry would each grab an end of hose, start pushing them together toward each other, then slip and bang their heads. Three minutes after our takeoff, everybody was shouting at once except me. I was afraid to interfere in this supposedly well-rehearsed maneuver for fear of receiving an excited, angry punch in the nose.

The hoses were finally all connected in one of those desperate last-minute-action moments of confusion. Every boy added gas to his balloon at once. Mr. M. dumped the water used to insulate the hydrogen tank off the platform with a trip of a foot lever, and the giant platform rose just in time to clear the mountaintop. We flew directly over the crater. Here, instead of being sucked downward by the vacuum as we had been in the Balloon Merry-Go-Round when the mountain was calm, we were greeted by a roaring swift upward blast of hot air which catapulted us far up into the sky. When we were about a half mile up, we were comparatively still. There might have been a little wind, but it wasn't strong enough to blow us off this hot sulphurous airshaft. We were trapped on top of it like those celluloid balls on upward streams of water in shooting galleries. Ladies and Gentlemen, we spent the night, a horribly long sleepless broiling night, on top of this volcano. The heat of the air from the crater and the altitude to which we were lifted caused the hydrogen to dilate in the balloons until they looked ready to burst. It was impossible to consider adding more hydrogen to the balloons in an attempt to get high enough to get off this airshaft and it would have been idiotic to let gas out of the balloons and thus lower ourselves nearer the inferno. The one relieving aspect of that miserable night was that the upward current of air kept the platform nice and level, though we swayed back and forth rather violently at times. The light from the blazing crater made everything up where we were bright red. This considerably intensified the heat. It was bad enough to be broiling without looking bright red too. This was indeed an ironic state of affairs: It was the highest any of us had ever flown and still we each had the feeling that this was closer to a sensation of hell than anything we had ever experienced before. I suppose too that our food was kept warm, though no one thought of eating anything that night.

We spent seventeen hours over the volcano, from five o'clock in the afternoon of the 26th until ten o'clock the following morning. At that time the shaft of hot air seemed to have lost its strength. We were lowered to an altitude of about one hundred feet above the mountain, or roughly fifteen hundred feet above sea level; and there a wind cleared us of that dreadful crater. The boys busied themselves keeping the platform level again, and the men and women of Krakatoa gave longing looks at their Island believing that the eruptions had ceased and that they had been foolish to leave. I cannot say that I shared this feeling at all. There wasn't a house left standing and I had no desire to return to this now desolate and fearful place even if the diamond mines were intact.

We flew until we were a mile over Java when, with stunning suddenness, the Island of Krakatoa in seven rapid ear-splitting explosions blew up straight into the air for as far as we could see. Our flying platform was rocked back and forth at thirty-degree angles by the concussions. Those of us who were near the balustrade hung on for life. A few of

those who were in the middle of the platform were tossed about like flapjacks in a skillet. We were twenty-seven miles away from the Island when it happened, which was just about far enough away for safety. Any closer and we would have been dumped right off the platform into the Sunda Strait. We couldn't see what was left of Krakatoa because it was wrapped in a thick huge tremendously tall black cloud of pumice, ashes, smoke, lava, dirt, with I suppose a few billion dollars worth of diamonds thrown in. We were fortunate in that the explosion was followed by a strong air current, produced in the same manner as waves on the surface of a lake when a stone is thrown in. We were swiftly being taken away from the scene of the eruption.

We were afraid that ashes, rocks, or even diamonds might fall on us and pierce our balloons, but all that actually happened of that nature was that we were soon enveloped by the thick black dust cloud which was so dense that it was almost impossible to see through, making it extremely difficult to keep the platform level. We traveled with this cloud for hours, not being able to see whether ground or sea was beneath us and fearing the horrible fate of crashing into a mountaintop in Java. We tied handkerchiefs around our faces so that we wouldn't breathe too much of the thick concentration of powdered ashes and pumice we were traveling with, and it seemed for a while that as long as the wind was with us, the powdered remains of Krakatoa would follow along and that we would be forever enveloped in this ghost of a dead island. The wind

generated by the explosion was tremendous and for the entire duration of this extraordinary journey we were hurtling through space at a fabulous speed.

The food situation, now that I look back at it, was the funniest I'm sure in the history of life-raft travel. We had three huge caldrons of a Dutch dish Mrs. D. had prepared for dinner the night of the eruption. This dish was called *Stampot von zuurkool met rookworst*. We also had a huge jug of Van Houten's cocoa and a crate of Gouda cheeses. I have heard of shipwrecked men living for days on hardtack and water, but we citizens of the former Island of Krakatoa lived on *Stampot van zuurkool met rookworst*. This was a dish consisting of meat cooked in gravy, sauerkraut, and sausages. Mr. M., the man who first discovered the diamond mines of Krakatoa and who persuaded the twenty other families to go and live there, felt responsible for them all at this moment of crisis. He supervised the rationing of the food, allowing but meager portions of *Stampot van zuurkool met rookworst* to each person and three swallows of cocoa with each meal. He also advised every family except one to jump off at the first sight of land, no matter what country it might be. "I have a good reason for this," he said: "Professor Sherman has no parachute. He will have to try and land the platform. It would be impossible and foolish for him to consider landing the platform on land, he will have to risk crashing it in some body of water. The family that volunteers to remain with him will help him control the balloons until water is sighted. They will then jump off, leaving the platform to Professor Sherman. I want every family except one to jump off as soon as possible so that as much food as can possibly be left over will be available to Professor Sherman whose journey over land might take him many days. With this in mind, the crate of cheeses, which are less perishable than the rest of the food, will be left intact for him."

I paid a considerable amount of attention to this speech of his in which I seemed to be leading man and most unhappy actor of a forthcoming melodrama.

Mr. M. then asked if any family wanted to volunteer to stay with me until the proper time was at hand for me to attempt a landing in the water. The F.'s volunteered immediately which cheered me up a great deal.

On the afternoon of the second day, the black cloud had thinned out sufficiently so that we could see that we were no longer flying over Java. I have since tried to reconstruct the voyage on the balloon platform and I believe we were flying at that time over the Indian Ocean. On the afternoon of the third day we sighted land and nineteen of the families gave forth with rousing cheers, embraced each other, and broke into happy dances. The F.'s ran to my side to comfort me, to show me that they had no intentions of leaving me until they had seen me safely to another body of water.

We were soon no longer over water but flying over thickly vegetated jungles. Mr. M. was leaning intently over the balustrade studying the nature of the country. He pointed out teakwood trees and sandalwood trees and observed the redness of the earth. "This is India," he said.

The nineteen families happily started readying their family parachutes. These were well designed; I shall describe them as best I can. There was a square silk sheet stretched out by two stout bamboo poles crossed diagonally from corner to corner. At each corner of the sheet was a parachute, and from each of these hung two straps attached to a belt harness. Each member of a family put on one of these belt harnesses, and when they jumped, mother, father, and the two children all descended together with the bamboo poles keeping them far enough apart so there was no danger of their bumping into each other in midair.

The families were all anxiously looking out for a nice spot to land on. At first we flew over nothing but dense jungle life, then we sighted a few small villages. Mr. M. advised everybody to avoid coming down in a village because the natives might not know what to make of parachutes. They waited until they saw a proper spot in the distance which was a rather soft-looking plateau, said goodbye to the F.'s and me, earnestly wishing us the best of luck, then all jumped at once so as to be together after they landed. The balloon platform lunged into the air when relieved of this weight and Mr. F., Mrs. F., F-1, F-2, and I continued on, a dreadful nine more days, which took us across India, Persia, Turkey, Hungary, Austria, Germany, Belgium, where the F. family finally left me, and took me on alone over England until I was at last able to crash the platform into the Atlantic.

William Pène du Bois

We had warm August and September weather and a magnificent wind, but except for the Dardanelles, which were too narrow to land in, we traveled clear across Europe missing every body of water. We missed the Caspian Sea, the Black Sea, and the Mediterranean. The five of us spent nine miserable days together, living mostly on cheese, rummaging through our barrels of food like dogs in garbage cans, separating the spoiled food from the good,

drinking rationed amounts of sauerkraut juice and stale cocoa, sleeping uncomfortably in four-hour shifts, and running around from balloon to balloon keeping the platform level until we thought we'd drop dead from exhaustion. On the ninth day we were over Belgium and we sighted the English Channel. I said goodbye to my friends the F.'s and helped them fix up their parachute. I sadly watched them as they dropped slowly to the earth below, then started to attempt to land the platform.

In order to get at the valves which release the hydrogen from the balloons, I had to break the hose connections with which they were attached to the tank. This, as you will recall, required a hundred-and-fifty-pound pull. I realized when I started to pull one apart that I didn't have enough strength left in me to do this fast enough to be able to land the platform in the Channel. I was afraid that the distance required to land the platform smoothly would take me clear across and I'd crash into the shores of England. So, tired as I was, I resolved to spend the afternoon flying over England. At seven o'clock at night, flying over Scotland, I sighted the Atlantic Ocean and started a tug of war with each hose until I got all of the connections apart. Then I started to descend.

My trip ended in a two-hour uphill run. Every time I let the gas out of one side of the platform, I'd have to run up the platform to the high side and let the gas out of that, then run back uphill to the other side, from end to end, across and back, to and fro on a perpetual incline until I

finally crashed into the Atlantic. I kept being reminded of a vaudeville act I had once seen in the London Music Hall. A Negro clown, dressed like a porter in a railroad station, played "God Save the King" running back and forth on the stage with hammers, striking the ties of the railroad tracks. One tune on this giant "xylophone" of his and he flopped on the stage exhausted as the audience rocked with laughter. I assure you I must have been awfully close to death when Captain Simon of the S.S. *Cunningham* sighted me and picked me up twenty minutes after my crash. The rest of my story you know, I believe. If you have any questions I'll gladly try to answer them.

The huge audience rose as one and acclaimed Professor Sherman with thunderous cheers and applause. After ten minutes of this hubbub, the Mayor, who had been wildly shaking the Professor's hand and patting him on the back, walked upstage and held up his hands to quiet the audience. "Have you any questions?" he asked.

There was a silent pause; then a man in the audience shouted, "How were you able to give us such a wonderful talk in your sickened condition, Professor Sherman?"

"*Ha, ha,*" shouted the Professor, leaping from bed. "I feel fine. I rested up completely on the Presidential train on my five-day trip across the country. I could have made the talk standing up, but when I saw this beautiful bed on the speaker's platform I thought I'd be a stupid fool if I passed it up."

The crowd laughed loudly at this, clapped its approval, then a woman stood up. "What are you going to do now, Professor?" she yelled.

With a broad grin on his face, Professor William Waterman Sherman rolled up his coat sleeves and showed his shirt cuffs. His diamond cuff links blazed and twinkled as they reflected the many rays from the footlights. "I have here a pair of diamond cuff links made simply of four diamonds the size of lima beans. They were given to me by my good friend Mr. F. the first day I landed on Krakatoa. I am going to first sell these cuff links, then build myself a balloon which I shall christen the *Globe the Second*. I shall attach to this balloon a basket house and a sea-gull catcher on which I am now working. Using food for ballast I plan to spend one full year in the air, one year of truly delightful living, a year in a balloon!"

About the Author

William Pène du Bois (1916–1993) published his first book when he was seventeen. Since then he has written and illustrated many beloved children's books, including the Caldecott Honor Books *Lion* and *Bear Party*, as well as *Bear Circus*, *Bear in Mind*, *Otto and the Magic Potatoes*, and *Peter Graves*. He was awarded the Newbery Medal in 1948 for *The Twenty-One Balloons*.